The
Find

Tom Flaherty

XULON
PRESS

This book is dedicated to my nieces and nephews who love to hear their Uncle Tom tell a story.

IMPORTANT DEFINITIONS

Microevolution - small changes that make for a variety of types within a species. i.e. There are many types of finches, yet they all have a common ancestor which is also a finch.

Macroevolution - large, complicated changes that can produce a whole new species from an existing one. i.e. Human beings and all living creatures have the common ancestor of a small single celled being in an ancient swamp.

Natural selection - the process by which evolution occurs. Nature, not any supernatural being, chooses only those offspring which are most capable of surviving. The weak die off while those most adapted to the environment continue on.

Punctuated Equilibrium - a theory proposed by leading paleontologists to explain the lack of transitional fossils after a hundred and forty years of searching. The theory maintains that macroevolution happened in relatively quick spurts (punctuations), followed by long periods with no change (equilibrium), and thus left few, if any, fossils of the links between species.

PROLOGUE

Comoros Islands, East Africa - 2002

*A*mericans are funny.
Kintu, a small African farmer, stood at the door of his shelter looking over his land in the early morning light. The Americans arrived at his island three weeks ago and began digging in the dirt and molten ash around Mount Karthala. Who knew how they got permission to be there? Some of the villagers worshiped the volcano. Many feared that digging at her base could make her angry. *And why were they digging for bones? What value is there in dried up old bones?*

Pineapples. Now there's something of value. This thought reminded Kintu of his responsibilities. In the 90 degree heat and almost 100% humidity, he decided he had better get going. People in the village needed pineapples and he had been the one to sell them in the market every morning, for years, until four days ago.

It was then that the American had approached him late one afternoon after finding that Kintu had learned English from the missionairies. The American asked him to look over the place where his team was digging because they had to leave quickly. He said he would pay one hundred United States dollars a day for every day they were gone, but Kintu would have to watch over the site day and night to make sure that it was undisturbed. He said they would be gone for three days.

This was no problem since his shelter was only a few hundred yards from where they were set up. His son could sell the pineapples, he supposed, and $300 was close to what he usually made in a whole year. He had shaken hands with the American and helped his group put blue tarps over everything at their digging site.

As he loaded his pineapples on a cart and began to pull towards the village he chuckled at what had happened next. When that group of Americans left, another American showed up at the site.

"No!" he told that American, "you may not dig here. The other Americans hired me. No one may disturb."

But this newcomer was not easily dissuaded. "I will take pictures," he said. "That way we can put everything back exactly the way it was."

What an amazing thing a picture box was!

The American took the African farmer's picture and showed it to him on a little screen to convince him that it could be done.

The answer was still "no." But then the American offered him more money than Kintu could make in ten years. *Where do people get this kind of money to spend on digging in dirt?* The American promised that it would all be back how it was before the other Americans returned and that no one would ever know. He also promised not to use any of the equipment the other team was using "because," he said, "that wouldn't be right."

Was it that wrong to let them dig for awhile if they put everything back? It seemed more wrong to reject money that could help his family for many years to come. Maybe his sons could go to school and become something more than he was? After much thought and anxiety he had taken the money. Somehow it didn't feel as right now as when he first got it.

Before sunset that day he helped the American remove the tarps and saw him take pictures of everything. Kintu inspected the American's pictures of shovels, picks, and brushes; and even of how the dirt was piled and where coffee cups were lying. That night the American was joined by several others. They brought their own equipment over and early the next morning they began digging.

After two hours of digging there was a lot of excitement in the group. They must have found something they were looking for. The group worked steadily for the next two days and even had lights to keep working at night. They used the pictures to put everything back. Kintu inspected the site. It looked unchanged. Then he helped the Americans carefully return the blue tarps.

Yesterday, the other American group returned.

"Did anyone disturb the site?" the American asked as he stood there with three one hundred dollar bills in his hand.

It didn't feel right to say "no," but what else could Kintu say?

That same afternoon, the other American group came back over and hugged the first American group as if they were long lost friends.

Yes, Americans sure are funny.

CHAPTER 1

Los Angeles - 2007

" *A* *nd now, the man you've all been waiting for. Five years ago he found the monumental micropteryx fossil, two years ago he authored the New York Times best-selling book, <u>The Ascent of Man</u>, and today he is the most compelling and prominent voice for the fact of evolution. Please welcome to the stage, all the way from Madison, Wisconsin, Dr. Derek Barnhouse!"*

To thunderous applause, Derek rose from his seat in the front of the auditorium and walked up the steps to the stage. He shook hands with his announcer, a respected paleontologist who obviously liked the feel of the microphone in his hand. As the man left, Derek stepped behind the lectern and looked out over the vast theater of faces. With a polite smile, he held up his hand for silence, and the applause reluctantly died out. But he was in no hurry to begin. Here he was, in front of thousands of young men and women of every race and ethnicity, and they were all there, eager and waiting to hear the truths he was about to impart. After a few moments of reverent silence, he began.

"Today I have one question for you, ladies and gentlemen. And that question may just change your life. This question,

and your answer to it, gives purpose to an existence that started in chaos. Now, some may tell you that existence started in perfection and has fallen into chaos, but simply put, they're wrong. Just look around you. Look at what we have accomplished. Compare yourself to your ancestors even a thousand years ago and ask yourself if there has been progress or regression. Humankind has not fallen from a perfect state into a mire; we have risen out of a mire into the complex beings we are today.

"A million years ago homosapiens evolved to a higher level than all other animals. While animals are driven only by natural instincts, humans developed a conscious mind that gave them the power to conquer, power to reason, power to love. For a time, the great responsibility of this mind drove many to invent gods and myths and religions in order to put the fate of their lives and the world in someone else's hands.

"But that age is coming to a close. Today a new breed of people is ascending. A people who are courageous enough to let go of the shackles of morality and religion. A people who are courageous enough to take responsibility for their own destiny. A people who are courageous enough to live as few have lived before. These people are not led merely by their instincts or by some crippling religion: they are guided by the logic of their minds. The choices they make are not about right and wrong, or about pleasing some unseen god, but rather about using the power of their consciousness. Those who are brave enough to live this way will survive and continue to ascend, so today my question for you is this..."

As Derek looked up to deliver the climax of his speech, he found himself unable to continue. He saw a man standing in the back of the auditorium, head and shoulders taller than everyone else. The auditorium lights shining on his white hair and the white silk robe he was wearing made it appear as if he were glowing. There was a thick band of gold around his chest that gave the appearance of ancient royalty.

The man was looking right at him. Derek knew he needed to finish — everyone was waiting — but for some reason the rest of the room fell away. He felt as if he were looking through a zoom lens on a camera and the face was suddenly right in front of him. The eyes, fierce but somehow serene, seemed to pierce his very core. As the man continued to stare, Derek felt a warmth inside of him that grew and strengthened until his whole body was shaking with a force he had never experienced before.

Power? Love? Life? There were no words for this. There was no category. Total acceptance and well being; yet completely beyond anything he had previously known.

But there was more. The man started smiling and the intensity increased until Derek felt like he was going to explode. He didn't want it to stop, but at the same time he couldn't take any more. He tore his gaze away from the eyes and began to scream, "Stop looking at me!"

Derek woke up trembling with his hands cradling his face. The sensation from the dream was still on him, although it was no where near the same level of intensity. He took a deep breath and tried to think clearly about the situation. What had just happened? He would never cease to be amazed at the capabilities of the human brain; his whole body still felt awash in warmth. Was that even possible? He made a mental note to ask a dream expert about the phenomenon. Who was that man? And why did he seem so familiar?

Derek rarely remembered his dreams, but this one consumed him. He tried to think of a name for the feeling that still had traces in his system. It was more than just love, more than excitement, more than wonder, more than happiness, more than strength, more than... everything he could think of. Finally he decided on a description that was as close as he could come: fully alive. More fully alive than he had ever experienced.

He took a deep breath and glanced at the clock on the hotel's oak bedside table. 3:03. It was the worst time of night to be awake, but sleep was out of the question. He rolled out of bed and emptied a small bottle of scotch from the Embassy Suites' well-stocked mini-bar into a cup of partially melted ice. He wasn't a drinking man and usually stuck with water, but recently he had found that just a little now and then helped him relax and concentrate, which was exactly what he needed at the moment. He took a sip and let the alcohol burn in his mouth a few seconds before swallowing. The last traces of the dream feeling went with it, and, relieved, he went back over to the bed. He knew he wouldn't be able to sleep, so, scotch in hand, he propped himself up on the pillows and switched off the lamp. He took another drink and thought about the feeling. *Fully alive. Have I ever felt like that before?*

The first thought he had was of his wife, Theresa. Making love to her definitely made him feel alive, especially in the early years of their relationship when they could barely wait to be alone after a night out. It was passionate and exciting, but compared with the dream it seemed so basic.

Then he thought of the birth of his first child. He would never forget the day Rachel was born. Theresa had been in labor for eight hours, and the doctor at St. Mary's had thought they might have to do a C-section. But she came out just before the decision was finalized, there she was - a messy, mewling bundle of perfection. On that day, Derek was speechless with wonder. But this still wasn't the same as the dream.

He took another drink, enjoying the fire flowing down his throat. Maybe his career had something close. Finding micropteryx, that day in Comoros, East Africa. Derek smiled. He remembered finding the first bone, and how chip by careful brush stroke, he and his team had slowly unearthed not one, but two nearly perfect skeletons of a reptilian bird, smaller and older than archeopteryx, with teeth in its bill and claws on its wings. It had since been called the most significant fossil unearthed in the last century. *That was exciting, but fully alive?* No, something without precedent had happened in that dream.

Now he remembered last week, when he had been playing "Texas Hold 'Em" with his colleagues on their monthly poker night. Derek chuckled at the memory. The table was down to him and Dr. Everett "Chip-on-the-Shoulder" Stone. Derek hadn't liked him since the day he came to UW Madison and tonight, Derek had refused to fold out of sheer defiance. There was no more betting since Stone had gone "all in." When he turned his cards, Stone couldn't help but gloat; he already had a flush in hearts. According to convention, Derek flipped his cards up as well revealing two pair, threes and fours. But there was still one card left to be dealt. The room was absolutely silent and then everyone gasped when David Jackson, another colleague, revealed the final card: the three of spades. Derek had a full house. An exhilarating feeling of triumph surged through him as Stone glared at him with hostility, stood up, and walked out.

Derek laughed out loud. *How do you compare a poker game to the birth of your first child?*

He emptied the last of his scotch. As he considered the dream again he knew there was really no contest. Those memories may have been drops, but the dream had been a plunge, a wave, a flood. It bothered him. *How can the most real experience of my whole life be in a dream? What does that mean?*

Then it came to him. The person in the dream must represent the next level in the ascent of man! He had been clearly superior to Derek; he hadn't even been able to continue speaking in the man's presence. That commanding presence, those oceanic eyes made all his efforts useless. Then a new thought occurred to Derek. *What if that man represents me? What if evolution has made another jump and natural selection has chosen me to ascend?* With that comforting thought, Dr. Derek Barnhouse drifted back to sleep.

CHAPTER 2

Derek was waiting to be introduced. He sat in the front row of UCLA's enormous Royce Hall and the place was buzzing with the energy of a standing-room only audience made up of undergraduates, faculty, and notable members of the area, waiting to hear his lecture. Since he had emotions on his mind, he realized that there would have been a time when this moment before speaking would have been enough to give him an adrenaline buzz, but it had become so routine, he didn't feel anything now except maybe a little hungry.

UCLA's president had invited him to come over a year ago to speak and she hadn't even flinched when Derek told her that his speaking fee was twenty thousand dollars. He didn't do it for the money, but he still demanded it because he felt like people valued the things for which they paid a high price. If he had been in it for the money he would have left the University of Wisconsin Madison a long time ago for the other offers he had received from almost every major university around the world after the micropteryx find. Madison paid him a base of $125,000 and allowed him, even encouraged him, to take as many speaking engagements as he wanted. They had waived any regulations about how much he could earn from outside sources. With almost monthly engagements like the one at UCLA and royalties steadily coming in from his book, he had reached a place where money had lost its meaning. Message was everything. Today he would do his most basic lecture that he titled: <u>The Fact of Evolution.</u>

Applause erupted after the president's introduction, and Derek rose from his seat and headed toward the stage. With his customary tweed jacket, T-shirt, blue jeans, and cappucino, he had always been a favorite with his younger audiences. Today would be no different. He climbed the steps and headed toward the lectern; it provided a nice spot for his cappuccino, but that was its only purpose since he no longer used notes. He liked to flow with the energy of his audience. He took a sip as he waited for the expectant hush. He smiled into the silence, took a deep breath, and began.

"Today I have one question for you, ladies and gentlemen. And that question may just change your life..."

As he continued with the introduction, he experienced a tingle of deja vu as he realized he was almost in exactly the same circumstance as the dream. He quickly scanned the audience to assure himself that there was no glowing man today and tried to shake off the feeling. The faces were different anyway, it couldn't be the same.

"My question for you today is this: 'Are you still ascending?'"

After getting the question out, he knew he wouldn't be stopped during this speech. Shaking off all remnants of uncertainty, he continued as confidently as ever.

"I can't tell you what a privilege it is for me to have an opportunity to share with you today on a topic that is the passion of my heart: the fact of evolution. Let me paint a picture for you. Pests attacking a crop of wheat are poisoned with insecticides. Only those with mutated DNA that have the advantage of resistance can survive and live to bear offspring.

Pretty soon the insecticides don't work any more because the pest it was supposed to kill has been wiped out, and another population of creatures has emerged in its place that has the trait of immunity. Natural selection allowed those that had the right DNA to survive, while those without it went extinct. This, my fellow scientists, is observable evolution that happens around the world every day. As many of you know, this is called 'microevolution.' After all, an aphid that can resist a pesticide is still an aphid. However, there is another type of evolution that I reserve the capital F "Fact" for: macroevolution. Macroevolution is the explanation of how all things around us have come into being. Close your eyes for minute."

Derek enjoyed the look of reverent sincerity as hundreds of eyes closed and silence filled the auditorium. He lowered his voice.

"Think about that aphid, but now go smaller, go farther. Go back in time to a primordial swamp where the right combinations of amino acids and proteins have finally connected to produce the first life on this planet. From this beginning a number of single-celled creatures come into being with a limited life span. As they reproduce, only those with DNA able to survive in the environment continue to repopulate. Some stay in a simple state of survival, others mutate and become something else, maybe a more complex form of amoeba. Forces in the environment make survival difficult for the new amoebas, just as our current insecticides do for the aphids. The amoebas are forced to adapt again and again and again. More complicated creatures come into being.

"Now think about four and a half billion years of this process. Eventually amoebas evolve into small invertebrates which diverge into vertebrates and more sophisticated invertebrates, and then fish arrive, followed by amphibians, and reptiles, then birds and mammals, some of which are the advanced primates that may have been the common ancestors of today's apes and, of course, us. Humankind. The capstone of evolution. But we're not done. Microevolution yields only variations within species but in the Fact of Evolution that I am addressing today, the possibilities are endless. So I will ask you again: 'Are you still ascending?'"

Immediately after the speech Derek was mobbed with undergraduates who had questions or wanted him to autograph their books. This was the price of setting up a book table in the atrium, but the truth was he loved it. If it was special to them, they might read it, and the book went so much farther than he could in an hour lecture.

"Dr. Barnhouse, Dr. Barnhouse." A brunette wearing a dangerously low white blouse approached with his book in her hand. "I don't know what you're doing now, but a group of us zoology students would like to treat you to lunch. Wanna' come?" Her eyes were filled with expectancy.

"I'm so sorry," Derek replied politely, "I need to go with the president soon, but let me sign your book. What's your name?"

"Darcy," she said leaning so close that Derek had to back away to sign.

He had seen her type many times before. At first it had been flattering to be the subject of so much attention. Now it was just one more thing he had to endure.

"Dear Darcy," he wrote, "I hope you never stop ascending. Derek Barnhouse."

As he handed it back to her she took the book and kept holding his hand. "Derek, I can't tell you what this means to me."

Derek wanted to laugh but resisted the urge as he freed his hand from her grasp. "I really do need to run Darcy. Have a good lunch."

Elaine Blake, the president of UCLA, finally managed to rescue Derek out of the swarm and into a waiting limousine.

Blake explained that the mayor would be joining them at lunch as well as a few wealthy alumni that might be willing to help sponsor a future dig.

"Derek, I want you to know that we're honored to have you with us today. Your lecture was fascinating. How do you do it without notes?" the mayor was asking at lunch.

Glad-handling had always bored Derek, but it was a cost of success.

"When I first stopped using notes," Derek began, "it was because I had memorized the lecture. But recently I find that I don't have to prepare anything specific. The direction I need to go for each unique audience just comes to me. I am as surprised as anyone by the way a lecture that I've given before might turn in a whole new way."

"Were you surprised today?" Blake asked.

"No, not really. This is my first time here, so I stayed with the basics."

"I always thought that evolution was only a theory. Has there been some break through that has changed that?" Blake questioned.

Derek chuckled. "Just because the scientific community uses the word 'theory' doesn't mean something isn't accepted as a fact based on evidence, which is why referring to evolution as a 'theory' is misleading to most people. That's one reason I lecture."

Elaine Blake didn't look convinced, but she let it go. Derek wasn't in the mood to elaborate, so he was glad when the subject changed.

"Professor Barnhouse, some of the alumni who have been successful in business would like to help fund a UCLA dig. We're wondering if you could lead a team seeking another missing link." Arthur Evans had made a fortune in oil before moving to southern California and had the air of a man who was used to being obeyed.

"It's not quite that easy, Mr. Evans. First, I work for the

University of Wisconsin and not UCLA, so any dig I was part of would have to include them. Second, micropteryx was a once in a century find. It would be wrong for me to get your hopes up."

Evans wasn't even interested in science. He wanted to be famous. Derek had seen this many times over. Once a person is rich, he finds that riches aren't enough, he wants more. He wants fame. And once he is both rich and famous? Well, he had found out that it still wasn't enough.

Derek's mind wandered back to his dream. Was the next step of evolution inviting him to become fully alive? The idea was intriquing to him.

CHAPTER 3

Madison, Wisconsin

As Derek pulled into his family's three acre estate on Madison's far west side he drank in the beauty of the tulips, hyacinth, daffodils and marigolds, as he drove from the front gate, around the man made pond, and all the way to their four car garage. The top was down on his BMW, and the air was filled with the scent of spring on this perfect day in late April. In a couple weeks the lilacs would be in bloom. This was his favorite time of year.

He and Theresa had purchased the place four years ago after he received a windfall from appearances on TV talk shows after the micropteryx find. For some reason everyone had had to talk to him right now, and they were willing to pay if he would accomodate them. No paleontologists since Richard Leakey and Donald Johanson had received this kind of international attention, and he hadn't minded, even though he knew it would pass as quickly as it came.

He couldn't wait to see Theresa. She was two years younger than him at thirty-seven, and had soft, raven black hair, with large brown eyes, and a body he knew her women friends envied. She was a part time pro bono lawyer who spent most of her time managing their home. He couldn't resist honking as he pulled into the garage. It was going to be a great night.

"Hey, hey, hey, Dad's home!"

Rachel made it to him first with a big hug. "Daddy, I missed you so much. Tell me you're not leaving again any time soon."

"I'm here Beautiful, and I don't plan on going anywhere ever again," he promised with a wink.

"Hey, Dad," Jared called from the grill. Derek walked to the deck and gave his neck a squeeze.

"Did you see any undergrads that might want to help tutor me?" Jared asked with a grin.

"There were so many that I think you need to come with me next time and do interviews."

"When do we leave?" was Jared's quick response.

Just then Theresa came in and his heart stopped. She had fresh color on her face from being in the sun, and was wearing a tank top and shorts with a smile on her face that made him feel like the luckiest man in the world. He felt like he was twenty again laying eyes on her for the first time. She walked over and gave him a slow kiss.

"Hey buddy, it's about time you showed up."

"I am so glad to be home, I can't even tell you."

"Well the steaks are on the grill and the potatoes are in the oven. I told the help to leave early because the Barnhouses need to be alone as a family."

Derek looked around at the immaculate 3500 square foot house. "Well they could have cleaned a little better, don't you think?"

"Dear...," Theresa laughed as Jared brought the steaks.

Later that night, Derek decided to tell his wife about the dream, and its possible meaning.

"It sounds to me like you might be having more of a mid-life crisis than some ascent to a higher level," Theresa stated

26

with brute honesty.

Derek smiled. Theresa could be blunt, but she was always totally honest. That had attracted him to her from day one. He pondered her comment, realizing it was exactly what he would say if he were in her shoes.

"I see it as an opportunity rather than a crisis," he replied with passion in his voice. "An opportunity to move beyond where I am to become something... more. Can you understand that?"

He could tell that she didn't even before she spoke.

"Derek, isn't it enough that you've made it to the top of your field, own a beautiful house, and have a family that loves you?"

It was a legitimate question, Derek knew. But the truth was that it wasn't enough. Not any more. The dream had touched the deepest part of him in such a profound way that he couldn't stop thinking about it. But he knew he couldn't come on too strong or he would scare Theresa away.

"Honey, all I'm saying is there is something about the man in the dream that needs to be explored and understood. It's hard to explain. He was superior without being pretentious. I should have been terrified; I could tell he could see right through me - there was no place to hide. I should have been terrified, but I wasn't. Overwhelmed, yes, but I felt somehow accepted. More than that, I felt chosen. I wanted him to be a future me, and frankly, I still want to believe that."

"I'd kind of like to meet him." Theresa responded in a way that meant she didn't want to talk about it any more.

"I hate to change the subject, but do you want to come Melissa's baptism tomorrow in Stoughton? I'm forcing the kids to go because it's a relative thing, and we just need to be there."

"You know it would feel like hypocrisy for me to step into a church. My message is in direct conflict with everything the church represents, even if Melissa is my niece.

Hopefully I'll be the one that will help her renounce her baptism when it's time to be confirmed."

"Is it hypocrisy to support my brother, even if you don't agree with the way he's raising his family? They know how you feel, so it would mean all the more if you were there."

"Jordan will understand why I'm not there, and he will already count it as an affirmation that I'm letting you and the kids attend."

Derek knew by the look on his wife's face that he was off the hook, and was glad. It was surprising to Derek that the church still persisted in western civilization after 2,000 years of chasing myths. The last thing he wanted to do on a free morning was go to a place he didn't believe in, and be with relatives he didn't get along with. Besides he needed to catch up on his e-mails.

Two hundred and fifty e-mails. Wow, they sure pile up when you miss a few days. Derek deleted most of them without even opening them, but what was this? "A Ghost from your past." He opened it.

Barnhouse,

The man I hired to watch over our dig during my son's funeral has cancer, and is not expected to live more than six months. He has confessed his sins. I know everything. I know about the $5,000 you paid him to keep his mouth shut. I know that you found micropteryx on our site and let the world believe you found it at yours. And I know how you put everything back in perfect order so that I would never find out.

Guess what? I found out, and I want my cut. By the way, thanks for the condolences. You stood there next to my dig and offered your sympathy to me over my son's death when you had just stolen from me the biggest find in history. What kind of a person are you?

I'm giving you a chance, Barnhouse. Here's the deal. Do what I say, or I go public. Wouldn't the papers and the talk shows love to get a hold of this one?

One million dollars by next Sunday, and 25% of the royalties of your best selling book that should have been mine. You have one week to get the million together. Do not disappoint me.

Yours truly,
Dr. Butch Radcliffe

Derek got up and immediately found the bottle of scotch he had hidden behind the dresser. Theresa didn't approve of drinking, and neither did he for that matter, but sometimes the situation demanded it.

How had some guy from a pineapple farm in Comoros, East Africa managed to get a hold of an obscure professor in the states to confess anything? And five years after the fact. *Unbelievable.* Derek took a long swallow of his scotch and remembered the event.

He had done what he had to do. Butch Radcliffe had been his roomate in graduate school and was a fraud and an opportunist. They had gone their separate ways, but somehow Radcliffe seemed to turn up in the exact place where he wasn't wanted. When Derek received word from his colleagues at Harvard that they were on to something - that their team at Comoros was getting close, but just couldn't stay any longer - Derek thought the invitation, and, more importantly, the exact coordinates were for him alone.

How Radcliffe got the coordinates remained a mystery to Derek. Maybe he sweet talked a research assistant, or, more likely, he bribed. Whichever, there he was when Derek's team arrived. There he was, digging in the exact spot where he wasn't wanted. There was nothing else to do but set up a dig elsewhere, out of Radcliffe's sight.

Halfway through their dig, Radcliffe's oldest son died in a car accident, and as their leader, he wanted the digging to stop while he attended the funeral in Houston. The team decided to go along, so they hired a man whose family lived in a shelter a stone's throw from the site to watch over the dig for the seventy two hours they would be gone. Derek had seen the opportunity.

At the time it had seemed like the only thing to do. Radcliffe was part of the archaeoraptor scandal of 1999 when it was discovered that fragments of a bird had been glued together with fragments of a dinosaur.(1) If Radcliffe had found micropteryx, Derek knew that authenticity would be questioned. He also felt sure that Radcliffe would not have donated the find to science, as he himself had done, but would have put it up for sale to the highest bidder. People like Butch Radcliffe gave paleontology a bad name.

Derek and his team talked about it and decided that for the sake of science they needed to at least try digging on Radcliffe's site while he was gone. He wouldn't have done it if the team had not been unanimous and emphatic.

The local at first offered resistance, but when Derek had raised the price to $5,000 cash, he yielded. Unbelievably, it was only two hours after moving their equipment to the site that they hit the first micropteryx. It took another two days and nights to get both skeletons out without doing any damage to the bones. When they were done, everything was put back exactly like it had been, and the ground shaped similar to the way Radcliffe's team had left it. The rest of the following night was spent moving their equipment back to the original site before daylight. Later that day they had gone over to Radcliffe's site to say how sorry they were about his son's car accident and to ask about the funeral.

They then waited a full week before revealing the find of

micropteryx and had pictures taken of the fossils delicately resting in grooves they made at their dig, so that there was a spot to point to when people wanted to know where the bones came from.

As Derek poured a second glass of scotch he found himself getting angry. He clicked on "reply." No one was going to blackmail Dr. Derek Barnhouse.

Radcliffe,

You left the wrong guy in charge of your dig and I took advantage of it. If you want to go public with this, have at it. Then I will be forced to tell the whole world why I needed to go to these measures for the sake of true science. Maybe I'll start by revealing the website you stole your doctoral thesis from. Archeoraptor exposed you as the fraud that you are. If you had discovered micropteryx, no one would have even believed it was real anyway.

One million dollars. Is that what you would have tried to sell micropteryx for? I'll be happy to give you all the money I received from the find. I donated it to the British Museum. I received nothing, and that's what you're getting too.

Barnhouse

Derek clicked send with a vengeance. In one way it felt good, and in another, something felt wrong. He poured himself a third glass of scotch, ignoring a thought that sounded to him like Theresa's voice, "A third, Derek?" Theresa wasn't going to dictate how he chose to live his life.

CHAPTER 4

I t was Monday night after a long day. Derek had cooled off a lot and tried to tell himself that he wouldn't be hearing from Radcliffe again. He and Theresa were sitting in the pool area chatting after supper when Jared and Rachel came over.

"Hey, Dad, Rach and I want to see the new Colin Farrell movie tonight. Any chance of us using the Beemer?"

"Why not?" Derek said with a smile as he tossed him the keys. "How are you for funds?"

Jared hesitated just long enough for Derek to get the clue.

"Alright, it's my treat."

It felt good to do something for his kids when he had to spend so much time away from them. He loved the fact that his teenagers liked being with each other.

"Have fun guys," Derek said, handing Jared a fifty.

As his children left, Derek noticed that something had fallen out of his wallet: a business card? As he reached over and picked it up he was immediately hit with the same warmth he had felt in his dream.

What is going on? he whispered to himself. He looked at the card with the feeling all over him. "Brian Patrick," where did Derek remember him from? *Oh, yeah.*

One week earlier he had done a guest lecture at the University of Wisconsin Milwaukee. It had finished late and when he tried to start his car the battery was dead. It had been raining when he left Madison, so his lights had been on, and because he had been listening to a book on his walkman he hadn't heard the warning beeps. Most vehicles today would have turned off automatically, but for some reason he hadn't been able to part with his '95 Mercedes when he bought the new BMW.

As he had looked under the hood and got out jumper cables, Derek remembered, he was approached by a guy in his fifties.

"Need a hand?"

"Yeah, I guess I left my lights on. Would you mind? I've got cables."

"No problem," the man responded as he held out his hand. "Brian Patrick, pleased to meet you."

Derek could feel strength as he shook. "Derek Barnhouse. Thanks for finding me."

After Patrick had made all the connections and the car was going again, he came over to the window. Derek rolled it down and looked up to say thanks, but it looked like the guy was troubled about something.

"You okay?" Derek asked.

"I'm sorry, but I feel I'm supposed to say something to you right now, and it's difficult."

Derek thought this was extremely strange.

"Go ahead, I'm all ears." *Why are there tears in his eyes?*

"You're coming into a time of crisis. It will shake you to the core, but there is a purpose."

"Whoa... relax buddy, I'm going to be just fine. Hey, thanks again for helping me," Derek said quickly as he began to roll the window back up.

"Would you mind taking one of my cards?" the man

asked, as he handed a card through the window. "Please feel free to call me, day or night, if you need someone to talk to in the days to come. And know that I'll be praying for you." This guy was so sincere that Derek simply could not bring himself to make his usual smart comment about religion. "Ahhh... Thanks a lot. Goodbye."

Derek had then driven away while manuevering his wallet out of his back pocket to put the card in. That was a week ago, before the dream and the threat, and now the feeling was on him again when he picked up the card. It was crazy, but he had to admit that he was shook up, and, "crisis," was certainly not far from what he was feeling. "Dr. Brian Patrick; Department of Philosophy; University of Wisconsin Milwaukee," is what it said, with an e-mail address, fax number, and several telephone numbers.

"Honey, are you alright?" Theresa asked as she came back outside. "You look like you just saw a ghost."

"I'm fine, but I'm going to have a scotch," he announced.

"Your hidden stash is going fast." Theresa knew more about Derek's drinking than either of them cared to discuss.

Hours later the kids were home and asleep, and Theresa, too, had drifted off at around eleven o'clock. A couple of drinks should have relaxed him, but the minutes ticked by on the clock and sleep simply would not come. The longer Derek tossed and turned, the more agitated he became.

Finally, at midnight, he decided to call Brian Patrick. Derek had climbed to where he was in life by taking chances, and Patrick had said, 'day or night.' He needed to do this or he would never know. After five rings, a voice answered with a sluggish "hello."

"Is Dr. Patrick there?"

"I guess that's me, if my brain's functioning correctly. What can I do for you at this hour?"

"Uuuuh, yeah, sorry about that. This is Derek Barnhouse, you jumped my car in the parking lot last Monday night. You told me a crisis was coming and at the time I thought, well, I thought you were a little crazy. Do you remember me?"

"Yes, of course I remember. It didn't occur to me until later that you were the Dr. Derek Barnhouse who had given the guest lecture that night. I wanted to attend your lecture because I had some questions about evolution, but I got tied up at the last minute. What can I do for you?"

There was no easy way to go about this, so Derek just plunged ahead.

"I have two questions for starters. How did you know that I was going to have a crisis? And you said the crisis had a purpose. What is that purpose?"

This question, Derek knew, went against everything he stood for. Evolution insisted on chaos and probabilities, there wasn't supposed to be a purpose for anything.

"Let's just say for now that when I was detaching the jumper cables from your car it became clear to me that very soon you would be in a crisis, and that something was dead inside of you, and that I was to play a role in helping you come to life, just like I did with your car."

Derek mildly sensed the warmth from the dream again, and was beginning to get excited. Maybe Brian Patrick was part of the next level to which human beings were ascending?

"Can I tell you a dream I had last week, without you thinking I'm crazy?"

"Absolutely. It would be a privilege; and don't worry, dreams have played a big role in my life."

Who was this guy? Derek wondered, and then began sharing the dream.

"It started with me being introduced to give a lecture.

After speaking a short time I noticed someone in the back who was wearing a white gown that seemed to be glowing under the lights. When I looked at him his eyes grabbed a hold of mine and pretty soon it was as if he was right in front of me. I was stunned silent. Everyone was waiting for me to go on, but I couldn't. There was something so commanding and gripping about those eyes that I thought he was a superior being, and as he looked at me I was filled with something that felt like liquid love. He was extending an invitation to me. I don't know why I know that, but I know there was an invitation. To what or where I can only speculate. Then I woke up. It was so real and alive that I couldn't think of anything to compare it with. The next day I spoke on the campus in a similar environment, and the funny thing is, I can barely remember what happened. Yet, I remember every detail of that dream.

Brian remained silent, so Derek finally asked, "well... what do you think?"

"That's a powerful dream," he replied cautiously. "Would you mind if I slept on it before responding?"

"No problem. Why don't you e-mail me, and ask your evolution questions as well. It's drderek@micropteryx.com."

"Wonderful... ," Brian said slowly. Derek could tell he was writing. "Sleep good, then."

"Goodnight."

When Dr. Patrick hung up Derek continued to hold the phone with his head spinning. *Did I just talk to an ascended man? Is he what I am becoming? Is evolution taking a step forward!* The possibilities were mind boggling.

However, it was late, and it was still possible that Brian Patrick was crazy, and that his own private emptiness and boredom were feeding a delusion. Derek knew he needed some sleep because the real world was waiting for him in the form of an eleven a.m. lecture.

CHAPTER 5

S cience Hall was one of the oldest buildings on the UW campus. There had been talk of tearing it down, but Derek was against it. He liked the feeling of being linked to the past.

As today's class filled the lecture hall he smiled to himself. It was his "Intro. to Evolutionary Theory" class, and this was the day he talked extensively about the fossil record. He had covered Darwin and his most famous works, <u>The Origin of the Species</u> and <u>The Descent of Man</u>, as well as the biogeographical, morphological, and embryological arguments for the theory, but he had saved the paleontological for last. He approached the lectern, faced his audience, took a sip of his tall double shot cappucino, and began.

"Good morning. Today, as promised, we will be digging into the fossil record." A few students groaned at the pun. "You may be surprised that Darwin's greatest opposition in 1859 was not from the right wing clergy: it was from the fossil experts. He wrote, 'The... gravest objection that can be urged against my theory is the fact that all the most eminent paleontologists and all our greatest geologists have unanimously, often vehemently, maintained the immutability of the species.'[2]

"Darwin claimed that the lack of fossils showing transitional forms was due to the fact that most bones are not fossilized and that much of the fossil record was not yet explored. He predicted that the fossil record would eventually show many of these transitional fossils if his theory were true. He said, 'The number of intermediate and transitional links, between all living and extinct species must have been inconceivably great.'(3)

"So what has the fossil record shown after 140 years of searching? Certainly not what Darwin expected. There are not just a few missing links, but rather, missing chains of transitional forms. The fossil record today looks much the same as it did in 1859 marked by two trends," Derek explained as he went to the chalk board.

1. <u>Stasis</u> - species exhibit no directional change, but stay the same once they appear until they go extinct; and
2. <u>Sudden appearance</u> - species appear all at once and are fully formed.(4)

"These trends led one of my mentors, Harvard zoologist Stephen Jay Gould, and his partner, Niles Eldredge, to advance a theory in 1972 called Punctuated Equilibrium. 'Equilibrium' refers to stasis; and 'punctuated' refers to sudden appearance. Gould, who before his death in 2002 was the preeminent voice on current evolution, called the lack of fossils showing a progression of evolution 'the most puzziling fact of the fossil record.' He called the extreme rarity of transitional forms in the fossil record 'the trade secret of paleontology.'(5) Eldredge explained in more detail the embarrassing coverup going on at that time. I quote: 'We paleontologists have said that the history of life supposes the story of gradual adaptive change, all the while really knowing that it does not.'"(6)

Derek loved to see the shock on students faces as he blasted away their preconceptions about the fossil record.

They needed to understand that science doesn't always fit in a neat little box. The lack of fossils didn't mean evolution wasn't true, it simply meant that the current understanding of it needed to be adjusted.

Many evolutionary biologists were dismayed by the fact that the fossil record didn't show the slow, gradual change which they felt was mandatory. Everett Stone had once confronted him vehemently: "We have shown that DNA is in all life, and that 96% of a chimp's DNA matches a homosapien's. Why can't you guys find the fossils for what we know is true?" Derek had laughed in his face and encouraged him to go get a shovel and start digging. Stone made it sound like he was personally responsible for discovering DNA, and that the lack of fossils was somehow Derek's fault for not digging hard enough. As a rule, people had a hard time letting go of their own preconceptions even when the facts stared them in the face.

Instead of helping his students resolve in their minds the seeming conflict between the fossil record and evolution, he decided to dismiss them early and assigned them some reading about Punctuated Equilibrium. They would talk about it together during Friday's lecture, but first he wanted them to wrestle with it alone.

That night was another family night, with pizza, followed by a video and popcorn. Rachel and Jared were both home, but Rachel seemed distant all night and went up to bed early.

"What's up with Rachel? She hasn't gone to bed at 8:30 since the fifth grade," Derek wondered out loud.

Jared continued to stare at the TV as if no one had said a word. It was Theresa who finally responded, "Maybe she's just tired because of all the added senior stuff she has to do. Why don't you go up and ask her? She could really use a little one-on-one Dad time."

Derek sat on the edge of the bed when Rachel looked up

from her pillow. It was hard for him to see his beautiful little girl growing up, but he sure was proud of the woman she was becoming.

"Going to bed already, Angel?" Derek asked as he leaned over and stroked her hair.

"Yeah, I'm bushed."

"Did you have something on your mind tonight? You seemed a little distracted."

She shrugged. "It was nothing."

"Okay, then tell me about nothing," he encouraged.

"Well, it's kind of about evolution."

"Perfect, that just happens to fall under my jurisdiction. What's your question?"

He smiled gently, urging her to open up.

"I don't know. The minister on Sunday was talking about eternity and how this life is just a womb preparing us for the next. I know we don't believe that, but I liked the thought of something more. What we believe takes us to the grave, then it ends. Life seems so short and so pointless."

Derek was instantly angry, but he knew he needed to control it. It wasn't Rachel's fault that she had heard that sermon at church.

"The reason people tell themselves there is an after-life is to avoid having to face reality in this life. Instead of really living, and facing the possibility of failure, they postpone living to some future time. The lie they believe robs them of the present life they could have."

"So maybe I don't want to face reality?" Rachel questioned.

"I think we're all afraid sometimes, Sweetheart. Courage is not the absence of fear, it's facing life inspite of our fears, and you are a very courageous young woman." Derek kissed her on the forehead.

"Thanks, Dad." Rachel hugged him and snuggled under her covers.

"Sleep well, and maybe we'll talk more about it tomorrow." Derek slipped out of the room and shut the door gently.

After he said goodnight to Jared and Theresa, Derek hurried to check for a response from Dr. Patrick.

There was an answer, but there was also a message from Radcliffe. Why had he aggravated him by calling him a fraud? He never should have responded so soon after drinking. *Well, I might as well get it over with,* he grunted to himself as he clicked on: "Money for Micropteryx."

Since you seem to be unreasonable, I have set up an appointment for Friday with Dr. Marilyn Becker to see how she views my demands. If you want to settle before then, she never has to know. I'm not going away.

Radcliffe

Marilyn Becker was not officially Derek's boss, but she was the dean of letters and science which meant she was responsible for overseeing many professors including those in the geology and zoology schools. She was a meticulous, by the book type of person and was merciless to anyone who broke rules. This was a bad development.

He was tempted to pour some scotch but resisted because he didn't want to develop the habit. His grandpa had been an alcoholic, and he knew addiction was in his genes, crouching at the door, if he started turning to the bottle for answers.

Derek wondered if he should talk to Theresa. She already knew about the micropteryx find and understood why he was forced to do what he did. But she was already in bed, and this would probably only make her worry.

Derek reached for his cell phone. He needed his lawyer.

"Why did you even admit the switch to him?" his lawyer, Parker Vanderbilt, wanted to know with frustration in his voice. "The local is nearly dead anyway, which means there would be no witnesses, only hearsay."

"I realize that, but then Radcliffe would come after my research assistants and put them in the horrible position of having to lie to protect me or tell the truth and feel like they're betraying me. What about the stuff I have on him?"

"It's something, but he has a lot less to lose since he's already been exposed as a fraud."

"So what should I do?"

"Meet with Becker alone first and explain everything you did. She will be angry, but maybe she'll come up with a plan to settle so that it doesn't have to go public."

"Maybe I should just pay him the million."

"Are you kidding me? If you do, you'll be blackmailed by him again and again whenever he needs the cash. Is there even legal documentation on his dig site?"

"It's unlikely. We just paid a few government officials and a land owner to do our dig. Africa is different than the United States."

"Well there you go. He's got nothing on you legally. However, the professional cost could be high, especially with all the publicity you've received. Meet with Becker and explain everything."

"Don't worry, I will."

Derek hung up the phone and slumped onto the couch. He knew he could catch Becker first thing tomorrow because she had office hours from 8:00-10:00 Wednesday mornings. He dreaded the meeting. Maybe he would have that glass of scotch after all.

Derek clicked on "Thoughts and Questions" from bpatrick@milwaukee.edu

Derek,

All I want to say about your dream for now is that I believe the man you saw was a higher being, and I think it is possible he was inviting you to become like him. The "fully alive" feeling you had may be the means of getting there.

Here are a few of my questions about evolution:

1. Doesn't evolution break the scientific law of biogenesis? Louis Pasteur established that life only comes from life. Doesn't spontaneous generation contradict that?

2. How do you reconcile macroevolution with the second law of thermodynamics? As you know that second law states that things left to themselves degenerate and go from order to disorder. Evolution has things left to themselves becoming better and more organized.

3. Where did DNA come from?

4. Why do most evolutionists seem to be anti-God?

Have a good night.

Brian

Derek was a little disappointed. It seemed like Brian knew something he wasn't saying about the dream. The questions about evolution were typical and fairly easy to answer, but he wouldn't do that tonight. He was totally drained.

Derek was on the platform again and was silent. The zoom lens was on, and the deep blue eyes were pouring love through him again. Just as Derek was about to turn away, the eyes changed to fire and the gaze lifted above him. Where there had been love, there was now anger. Terrifying anger.

Derek turned his head and lifted his eyes to see at what the burning eyes were glaring. There was a grotesque being hovering right behind him, large and black, with a hideous gargoyle like face. Derek felt a cold blanket of fear mixed with disgust coming over him. His whole body began shaking with terror. He needed to get away from this being quickly, but he couldn't seem to move.

There was a defiant smirk on its face as it tried to hold eye contact with the eyes of fire that were staring. For all of his size and seeming pride, Derek could see fear in the gargoyles eyes and a slight trembling of its whole being. What was this thing and why was it right behind him?

CHAPTER 6

When Derek woke up the next morning the first thing he did was replay the dream again and again. The fear he felt was almost as real as the warmth from the previous dream. He'd ask for Brian's take on it in tonight's e-mail, but right now he needed to shake it off, and get ready for work and his meeting with Becker.

Derek didn't like Marilyn Becker's office. It was too neat. The books were lined up largest to smallest and there wasn't a stray paper on the desk or even a coffee cup. Becker wasn't the type to have a noticable vice.

After telling her everything about the micropteryx find, she was angry, and on the verge of losing control. Derek had never seen Marilyn Becker like this before.

"What you did Doctor Barnhouse was not only unethical and stupid, it was also highly unprofessional. You leave me with no choice except to report you to Chancellor Stoltenmeyer to find out how he wants me to proceed."

"Do I need to remind you, Marilyn, that you approved what I did?"

"How dare you accuse me!" she was really getting hot now. "What could possibly lead you to make so outrageous an accusation?"

Derek took no pleasure in this, but it was clearly

necessary. He slid two e-mails from 2002 across Becker's desk. "You were an assistant dean overseeing our department at the time," he reminded her.

Becker read in silence.

Dr. Becker,

We have a unique opportunity in the next 72 hours to dig on the most desirable spot in this region. This was the area we came down here for, but another team beat us to it, paying off the locals. For $5,000 we can have full access to this site for a brief window of time, but the clock is already ticking. I questioned if we were crossing into a gray area, but after discussion, the team has come to a consensus that it is important for us to take advantage of this hopeful possibility for the sake of science. Please let me know if our department will approve this amount. You will not regret giving the OK.

Barnhouse

She now put the other e-mail on top and began reading with increased intensity.

Dr. Barnhouse,

I am leaving for San Francisco this afternoon and still haven't packed. We do have a pool of undesignated grant money for emergencies, but I'm going to have to trust your judgment in this case. You're putting me in a difficult position because there is no one here right now to confirm my approval. I hope the money is well spent.

Becker

Derek could tell that she understood her responsibility in what he had done. She didn't seem as angry as before, but looked more determined than ever.

"Do you realize what happens if this gets out?" she finally asked.

Derek didn't know for sure if this was rhetorical, or if she wanted an answer. Before he could speak she went on with intensity.

"I'll tell you what happens. Your name becomes stained, all you've accomplished becomes stained, and the good name of this university becomes stained. Do I have to remind you that in the area of science trust is everything? If we aren't credible in the world's eyes, no one will trust our science."

"I am really sorry about this whole mess, Marilyn, and I assure you that I would never use those e-mails against you. Please know that I never imagined it would come to this."

"Sorry, won't be good enough, Professor Barnhouse." She paused as though she were in deep thought. After awhile she looked up at him again.

"How much did you make on that book?"

It was a demand more than a question. "About a million up front, and now the royalties are running about five thousand a month."

"Bring your checkbook on Friday, and your lawyer. I want you two to settle this thing and both sign a waiver of silence before it goes any further."

"You mean we're going to pay him off?"

"No. You are simply going to settle with Radcliffe out of court and out of the press. You're going to have to pay for your misdeeds, Professor. You'll have to give him something up front, but mainly I want you to sign over all future royalties to your book. That way he'll prosper only if your name continues unsullied."

Derek resented being ordered around. He was a world famous paleontologist, and their whole university had enjoyed the spotlight because of him. He knew Becker was afraid that the spotlight would be on all of them again, for the wrong reason. As much as he hated it, he knew she was being reasonable.

"What time on Friday?"

"I meet with Radcliffe right after lunch. We'll be ready for you at two o'clock."

"I'll be there with my lawyer."

After his morning lecture Derek was doing a job interview for his head research assistant position over lunch. He had interviewed a young man on Friday that was well qualified, but in a day of equal opportunity he thought it would be good to interview a woman as well.

Tutto Pasta was an Italian place at the end of State Street that had great food and a wide open atmosphere that would have to serve as the equivalent of keeping his office door open. He rarely met with a student over lunch but this was the only way he could fit the interview in today and he wanted it over with.

It would be a quick, professional interview and would probably end with a pleasant rejection note next week, he thought. Derek's secretary had told him her name was Marie Chandler, a twenty five year old, who had been working as a research assistant at Harvard for the last two years and had just transferred to Madison to be close to her ailing mother.

When he arrived, the place was packed, but the hostess seemed to recognize him through the crowd.

"Dr. Barnhouse, a Ms. Chandler has already arrived and wanted me to look out for you." Her eyes were staring as if he should know her. Derek drew a blank.

"You don't remember me do you? I was in Geology 303 with you last year. It was my favorite class."

"You do look familiar," Derek smiled. "Now where is Ms. Chandler?"

She led him to the table, gave him a menu, and said she'd be right back with the coffee he'd requested.

After squeezing into a chair and looking up, Derek had to stop himself from staring. The woman sitting across from him was drop dead gorgeous. White blonde hair and beautiful turquoise eyes, set off a face so stunning it didn't need make up.

"Hi, I'm Marie," she said while reaching out her hand.

"I'm Dr. Barnhouse." Why did he sound nervous? *Grow up,* Derek scolded himself. *You've seen beautiful women before.*

"I just want you to know, Dr. Barnhouse," Marie started off, "I feel like I already know you. The professors at Harvard all remember you well and refer to your success as an inspiration to young students. I've read The Ascent of Man twice and try to stay current on your published articles."

She smiled at him as she said this, and it melted his defenses. He hated himself for it. She was blonde, but there was no dizziness here, nor was there anything flirtatious. She was clearly intelligent and held him professionally in high esteem. He wanted to tell her right now that there was no way he was going to hire her because she was too beautiful. The job would often require the assistant to travel with him and it wouldn't look good, and Theresa wouldn't appreciate it either. But then there were all those discrimination laws. Had anyone ever been discriminated against for being too attractive?

The waitress came back and took their orders. Spaghetti and meatballs for him, an Antipasto salad for her; he wanted coffee, she stayed with water only.

"Feel free to call me Derek," he began after the waitress left, wondering what happened to the professional distance he had planned to maintain. "Tell me what professors you had at Harvard."

After a few laughs together about common professors they had studied under, Derek began thinking of the price she had paid to be back here near her mom. He found his heart filled with sympathy.

"Is there something wrong?" she asked.

"Marie, I heard from my secretary that your mom is very sick. How is she doing now?"

Tears came to Marie's eyes. "I'm sorry," she whispered, as she wiped the tears with her napkin, "I'm actually doing okay with this, but it was just so sweet of you to ask. She has terminal cancer, and next week they're moving her hospital bed home and having hospice come in. Dad will be her full time nurse, and I came home to be able to relieve him from time to time."

Derek wanted to go over to her side and comfort her. What was wrong with him? This was a job interview and she was an applicant. Fortunately the waitress returned at that moment with their food giving Derek a chance to get a grip on himself.

After a few minutes of silent eating, he forced himself to move things to safer ground. "So, tell me why you feel you're qualified for this job?"

As Marie began a litany of accomplishments and experiences she had had, Derek analyzed his feelings. This was not like him. He had always let his mind and will rule over his emotions even with adoring undergrads around him in every city he visited. He never felt anything for them. Theresa was amazing, so he never looked around. It didn't even occur to him.

Whenever Marie paused, he would ask an appropriate question, but he was mostly fascinated by his response to her. He was in a crisis. He hadn't been sleeping well and those dreams had awakened something in the depths of his being that he was having trouble getting rid of.

"Professor Barnhouse... ," she smiled. "I mean Derek,

could I be frank with you?"

"Please do."

"Besides my qualifications, and the privilege it would be to work for you, I just really need this job. It would give me the pay and flexibility I need to help with my mother, and allow me to continue my studies. What do you think?" she asked with no guile at all.

"I think you're hired," Derek heard himself say as he reached across the table to shake her hand. "I'll look for you first thing tomorrow morning. Training starts at eight."

That night Derek arrived home early and told Theresa to get her best dress on because he was taking her out. After a romantic dinner at The Edgewater, they went down to the Union for ice cream and then walked along the lake front.

"I hired a new research assistant today."

"The grad student you interviewed last week?" she asked. "What was his name again, Holmes, or Homan?

"Homer. No, I decided against Rich even though he's been on my team for the last two years. The young lady I hired is from Harvard and just transferred back here because her mom has cancer."

"Honey, is it smart to pass over those who have been loyal to you for a newcomer? Won't the team resent her?"

"I'm hoping not. But maybe I'll find some other paid position for Rich and give him a new title, just to be safe."

"What's she look like?"

Derek silently bemoaned the fact that women always had to know about each other. "She's attractive, I suppose, but she's very into her research and I don't think she's got much of a social life."

"Will she travel with you?"

"Possibly from time to time, as the job requires, but you're always free to come along if you think it would look bad."

"I guess most people today don't even think about that,

but wives still do."

They walked for awhile before she spoke again.

"Derek, I'm concerned about how little time we get together, this is the first real date night we've had in months."

"I thought we were talking about the new intern. Theresa, don't you trust me?"

She looked into his eyes, "I want to trust you, and I think I do, but I don't like the idea of any woman spending time with you especially when we get so little time alone."

"Have I ever let you down?" he asked with a smile.

Before she could answer he was kissing her, first gently, and then with passion.

After returning home and making love to his wife, Derek wondered if the whole night was a response to the guilt he felt over his infatuation with Marie. After Theresa fell asleep, he retreated down to his study and tried to get his mind off of complicated matters like women and motives.

He began his e-mail to Brian by relating the previous night's dream in detail. It felt good to tell somebody who wouldn't laugh and who might be able to give some feedback as to what was going on. His e-mail went on:

> Please let me know what you think about this dream, and don't feel like you have to hold anything back. As far as your questions on evolution, let me take a shot at it in as simple of terms as possible.
>
> 1. The law of biogenesis. It might interest you to know that the one thing Darwin didn't cover in <u>The Origin of the Species</u> was the origin of the species. He never made a case for spontaneous generation, nor did he rule out the possibility that a supernatural being deposited life on this planet before abandoning it. Fred Hoyle, a famous as-

tronomer and mathmatician in our day once addressed his evolutionist collegues about the odds of spontaneous generation occurring. He said the probability of life rising by chance is the same as the probability of rolling six on a die five million times in a row.(7) Evolution does not explain the origin of life but only the process by which that life led to the wonderful variety of living things we witness today.

2. The second law of Thermodynamics. Based on the radiometric dating of rocks, geologists estimate the age of the earth to be 4.6 billion years. That's a lot of time, and with enough time anything can happen, and in fact, evolution clearly has happened.

3. DNA. I'm sure you're familiar with the story of Antony Flew. He was one of the most influential atheists in the world until he changed his position a few years ago to become a theist.(8) The main reason, I understood, was the nature of DNA, and that there is no known natural process capable of producing information. "It takes intelligence to produce intelligence" is how the argument goes. Once again, evolution does not rule out a supernatural intelligence leaving something here on this planet billions of years ago at the beginning of everything. Hoyle has even proposed the possibility of aliens from space leaving DNA here before evolution took over.(9) I'm not sure how DNA got here, but I do know that it is in all living things showing the biological relationship we have to all of our ancestors down to the first cell that had life. We have marvelously ascended to where we are

today, and that process is still occurring.

4. Anti-god. Darwin never called himself an atheist, he preferred agnostic, because he didn't know how the world got here, or even life. Science doesn't cover those questions. What Darwin observed was the world that was already here. Some of his friends felt that there was a loving, all-knowing and all-powerful god watching over his creation; Darwin believed differently. Some tried to justify man's suffering by saying that it served his moral improvement, but Darwin noted the suffering in nature as well, and it led him to question whether there was a god.

"What advantage," he asked in Origin of the Species "can there be in the sufferings of millions of lower animals throughout almost endless time? This very old argument from the existence of suffering against the existence of an intelligent First Cause seems to me a strong one; and the abundant presence of suffering agrees well with the view that all organic beings have been developed through variation and natural selection."[10]

After the death of his eleven year old daughter, Annie, he gave up all faith in the god of the Bible. He wrote to his geologist friend Charles Lyell, "I would give nothing of the theory of natural selection, if it requires miraculous additions at any one stage of descent."[11] His theory was natural selection instead of god. He wanted nothing to do with any explanation that required a supernatural being helping the process at any point. Evolution by natural selection rules out any god who is still present.

You, as a philosopher, must certainly understand

the host of challenges to an all-powerful, all-benevolent being in the modern world. Any god who would allow all of the atrocities of our day has a lot to answer for.

Derek

CHAPTER 7

D erek turned his phone back to ring after his three o'clock lecture on Thursday and noticed he'd missed a call from Theresa. He only had to wait one ring for her to pick up.

"Hey Hon, what's up?"

"Oh, good, you called back. Can you come home early tonight?" She sounded uncharacteristically deperate.

"What's going on, Theresa?"

"There's something wrong with Rachel. After school she came home and was real edgy. When I asked what was wrong, she insisted that it was nothing. When I went to her room later to check on her she had been crying but still wouldn't talk. Later, while putting away clean clothes, I distinctly heard her say to a friend on the phone: 'Sometimes I don't even know if life is worth living.'"

Derek was supposed to have office hours now and had been hoping for few students and a chance to relax. The last thing he needed was a crisis at home.

"Theresa, that's just an expression. I hardly think a teenage girl crying could be classified as an emergency. She's under a lot of stress and probably just needs a little space."

"Rachel doesn't cry, Derek. You know this must be serious."

"Yeah, but when she's stressed out 'serious' can mean a B on an assignment; or a friend not talking to her in the hall;

or it could simply be her time of the month. I can't come running home everytime someone's got the sniffles, T."

"How many times have I asked you to come home early?" The voice was steady, but Derek knew she was seething. "You live in your own little kingdom while I take care of everything at home and take care of my clients. I am here while you travel all over the world and then I ask one little favor of you and you lecture me like a two year old. Nevermind, Dear," her voice dripped with sarcasm. "I forgot you're too important to be imposed upon by something as trivial as your own daughter's emotional health." He heard a violent click and the line went dead.

Yikes, Derek thought, *what's wrong with her. Does she even consider the stress I'm under?* He had a job and it had requirements and the university paid him a salary for fulfilling them. Why was that so hard to understand? She came and went to her job as she pleased and did most of the work for free anyway. It didn't bother her to live in a beautiful house, nor did she complain when he took her along to Europe at least once a year. His work was what paid for those amenities. *I'm going to stay right here for the full two hours my job demands,* Derek decided with rising indignation. *Then I'll go home to talk with Rachel.*

Ten minutes later Derek called his colleague, David Jackson. David was a tall, African American who taught geology, and was a favorite with students. In Derek's opinion he was one of the most brilliant minds as well as one of the most engaging lecturers on campus.

"David, are you there?" it sounded like he was on a speaker phone.

"Yep, what can I do for you?"

"I've got a situation at home, and I'm wondering if you could cover my office hours this afternoon. I would be in your debt."

"How about some mercy at the next poker night?"

"Not a chance, but I'll be glad to put the first ante in for you."

David chuckled and said, "You do whatever you need to do. I'll be glad to cover for you."

"Thanks, man. I owe you one."

When Derek arrived home he went right upstairs to find his daughter. He didn't know where Theresa was, but he wasn't surprised she hadn't met him at the door with a kiss.

Rachel was a senior at Edgewood, a private high school on the west side of Madison. She was on the way to being valedictorian and had already been accepted into Harvard, Derek's alma mater. Although she was generally well-liked, she hadn't dated much because she saw all the misery her friends went through with boys. It really was uncharacteristic of her to have an emotional breakdown.

Derek tapped on the door and let himself in. Rachel was sitting at her efficiently organized desk doing homework and listening to her ipod nano while doing homework. After taking her headphones off, she looked up revealing red, swollen eyes.

"Hey, Beautiful, what's up?"

"You're home early."

"Yeah, I wanted to check on you. Mom said you were crying earlier and didn't know why. She thought you didn't want to tell her."

Rachel rolled her eyes. "It's not like it's an emergency. You guys worry too much. I'm fine."

"Well, I'm here now," Derek shrugged, "so you might as well tell me."

"Gosh, why do parents always have to know everything their kids are going through? Isn't dealing with things alone part of growing up?"

"No, part of growing up is learning to share your problems with those who love you, so that they can help you," he said gently with a smile. "C'mon Rach, what's going on?"

"Fine." She turned her chair to face him. "It's about evolution again. It's just so depressing. I am a completely random person with no purpose for being. The only difference between me and an earthworm is chance. I have no future except old age and death. If I reach my goals, who really cares? And if I don't, so what?"

After a short pause, she nodded as if to herself and said, "Yep. That's about it. Nothing to worry about, just like I said."

"Oh, Honey," Derek's heart broke for her. "Those are some tough questions."

After several moments of silence he ventured: "Do you remember how Neo had to choose between two pills in the Matrix?"

Rachel looked up and nodded.

"He could either take the blue pill and go back to the comfortable lie he was living in, or he could swallow the red pill and face the truth. But whichever choice he made would define him the rest of his life because he'd never be able to go back once the decision was made. He chose the truth and lived his life courageously fighting for others who were believing lies.

"Rachel you have chosen the truth and you're suffering for it, like Neo. I can't deny any conclusion you've come to, but I can promise you this: I've got your back and so do Mom and Jared. We will journey every step of the way with you and promise to never lie to you."

With tears in her eyes, Rachel leaned into a hug. "That means a lot Dad. I'm sorry about this. Maybe it's because graduation's coming and I know I'll be moving away soon."

"Wherever you go, we're going to be here for you." The truth was that Derek didn't know what he was going to do when Rachel moved away. She was more than a daughter to him; she was one of his best friends.

Supper that night was strained. Jared was out with friends, Rachel was quiet, and Theresa still seemed angry. Every effort Derek made at conversation was politely answered but never added to. After the meal he cornered Theresa as she loaded the dishwasher.

"So, am I out of the doghouse?" he asked. She didn't look up. "I came home early, didn't I?"

"What do you want? A medal for showing a little concern for your children who need you?" After a tense silence she looked up and he knew it wasn't over. "You have the nerve to wonder if you're some type of ascended being, and all I'm asking for is some basic human respect. Is that too much, Doctor Barnhouse?"

"I'm sorry for not being perfect. I've been under some stress myself, you know."

She softened a little. "I'm sure you have been. And I am grateful that you talked to Rachel. I just don't know what to do with her sometimes."

After a brief silence she asked, "Would you mind if Michelle and I went out for coffee tonight? We want to discuss graduation parties together."

"Go for it. I've got plenty to do."

Derek pushed open the swinging doors and made a beeline through their large Victorian dining room and plush living room to the sunken family room where he collapsed on his favorite chair. He needed to relax. Where had all the tension come from between him and Theresa? And why did Rachel pick right now to start asking the hard questions that had no good answer?

The dream. Derek jumped up out of the chair and headed to his office. He needed to know what the dream meant.

He was happy to see Brian had gotten back to him so quickly.

Derek,

Before we get into the dream, I want to respond to your thoughts about evolution. Is it possible that Darwin brilliantly observed the science of microevolution, variation within a species, and then expressed not science, but his faith against God, when he took the leap to macroevolution, suggesting that all species evolved from a common ancestor?

You admitted that the possibility of a supernatural being was actually more rational than believing that life rose out of non-life, and that it probably took intelligence to create the information in DNA. Your point about length of time overcoming the second law of thermodynamics is possible, but it is not science. Science says it can't happen, but if one believes in macroevolution, then he must believe that it did happen, even though how it happened can't be explained.

Darwin's observations of suffering in nature and the conclusions he came to about God's existence from them had nothing to do with science either, only his lack of faith. He didn't want to believe in a God that would needlessly (in his eyes) let suffering occur to animals and who allowed his daughter Annie to die. It seems to me that instead of turning to God in his grief, he rejected him completely and dedicated his life to a theory that doesn't require a Supreme Being.

Today macroevolution is taught as science by giving examples of microevolution as proof. I don't care if people believe in macroevolution, it's a free country, but I think it's dishonest to pass it off on society as science, when it is really only a theory that takes large leaps of faith to believe.

Thanks for putting up with my opinions.

Now to the dream.

Does this sound like the man you saw in your dream?

"I saw... one like a son of man dressed in a robe reaching down to His feet, and with a golden sash around his chest. His head and hair were white like wool, as white as snow, and His eyes were like blazing fire... "

That's from the last book of the Bible called Revelation. It's found in chapter one verse fifteen and it's a description of the risen Lord Jesus Christ. I think the dream you just had is about a spiritual conflict between light and darkness with you in the middle. What do you think?

Brian

Derek resented the fact that a philosophy professor was presuming to lecture him on evolutionary theory. It was also a huge disappointment that Brian was clearly a traditionalist who still believed in the Bible.

On the other hand, Dr. Brian Patrick was an intelligent man. He actually made some good points about macroevolution, even if they were uncomfortable to consider. And the description he gave did match the person he had seen in his dream. It was still early. He decided to call.

"Brian, this is Derek. How are you tonight?"

"I'm good. How are you?"

"Well, to be frank, I was troubled by your e-mail."

"How so?" There was no defensiveness in Brian's voice.

"Well, I didn't figure you as the kind of person that believed in the Bible, a book full of contradictions that gives the age of the earth as six thousand years." Derek knew he sounded harsh, and he didn't want to be, but he had to know.

"What contradictions?" Brian asked innocently.

Derek was embarrassed. He didn't actually know the specifics - he had only opened a Bible a few times - but people he respected said that there were contradictions and he had taken their word for it.

"You have me there," he finally replied. "I honestly don't know much about the Bible and don't know any contradictions first hand. I'm a victim of hearsay. But how about the age of the earth?"

"Geneologies trace Adam and Eve back to about 6,000 years ago, but many people interpret Genesis in a way that allows for a much older earth."

This shocked Derek. "Really? I'd be interested in hearing about that."

"Do you ever get to Chicago?" Brian asked, seemingly off the subject.

"Actually, I'm speaking next week on the Northwestern campus. Why?"

"I've got a friend down there I'd like you to meet: Dr. Charles Crowder. He is a Hebrew scholar who helped with the 1973 translation of the New International Version of the Bible and is passionate about an old earth interpretation of Genesis 1:2. He would also be fascinated to hear about your dreams. I know you would enjoy talking to him if you could make time for it."

"Okay, I'd love to. Get me his number and address and I'll look him up. Should you call him first to make sure it's alright?"

"I'll be happy to, but don't worry, it won't be a problem. And Derek, before you visit with him you might want to read over the first chapter of Genesis a few times, so that he doesn't lose you when he gets going. And trust me, he will get going."

"I'll do it. Thanks Brian."

"Anytime."

Derek didn't know where he was going to find a Bible. He vaguely remembered Jared saying something about getting one at school from a man who was passing them out in the parking lot. Jared had taken it out of respect for the old man who gave it to him, but Derek had no idea where he would've put it.

Derek slipped into Jared's room. He could still hear the TV in the background, so he felt like he was safe. He needn't have worried; the small book was easily visible on top of some old CDs. Derek felt like a thief as he delicately lifted the small volume and slipped it into his back pocket. He carefully made his way back down to the study.

After finding the book of Revelation from the table of contents, he began to read and didn't want to stop. He was surprised he found it so intriguing. He had grown up in the Unitarian Church where the standard fare on a Sunday morning was a poem, a few verses of "Morning Has Broken," and a message on a book someone had recently read. People who believed the Bible was literally true were looked on as naive and simple minded.

Jesus was intense, and the judgments he read about in this book were consistent with the terrible anger he remembered in those eyes of fire. Near the end of the book was a wedding between Jesus and the bride as well as a description of a worldwide war followed by a new heaven and a new earth.

Did Christians think this was really going to happen? Probably a few fundamentalists did, Derek thought, but they also thought Barney the purple dinosaur was a tool of Satan. People like Brian most likely thought the book was a metaphor of the battle between good and evil.

It was midnight when Derek was done with Revelation. It was funny, but he was more awake than when he started. Maybe he should find Genesis and at least get a start on his reading assignment. He started paging through the small book but couldn't find it! He looked in the table of contents and there was no Genesis; the first book was Matthew. He laughed at himself. This was only a New Testament. He'd have to find a whole Bible tomorrow.

CHAPTER 8

O n his way out of an ethics committee meeting the next morning Professor Everett Stone pulled Derek aside.

"I saw you walking with your new assistant yesterday. Do you really think it helps the academic atmosphere to have a model strutting around here?"

Derek was shocked at how overt Stone's bitterness had become. It had embittered him to have Derek find micropteryx and author a best selling book while he was stuck in the same rut he'd been in for twenty five years. But Derek always tried to be polite since Stone was twenty years his elder.

"Well, I'm sorry, Everett, but she's well qualified and I needed to fill an important position. Are you prejudiced against her because she happens to be attractive?" Derek knew that everyone on campus had to stay far away from even the appearance of discrimination.

"All I'm saying is that I suspect her good looks didn't hurt in qualifying her." Stone didn't want to let go of it.

"Marilyn cleared it, so complain to her if you want," Derek said, controlling his anger as he left the room.

He was tempted to bring up her Harvard background which would have blown Stone's top. Stone had applied to Harvard for graduate school and been rejected, so he enjoyed painting Derek as an arrogant know-it-all. It was one of many sore points between the two of them, but it didn't really matter: they didn't have to be friends, they just had to share a campus, and serve on little committees together once in awhile. Stone could waste his life chewing on petty little issues if he wanted to, but Derek didn't have time for it. Right now he needed to prepare for his "lecture/discussion" on Punctuated Equilibrium.

As about sixty students gathered for the eleven o'clock lecture, Derek took time to look around the room. The university brought top students from almost every nation. These were young people who would go back and be leaders in their respective countries and influence the global issues that would face their generation. What a privilege it was to speak into their lives.

When everyone was seated he rose from his desk, took a drink of his coffee, and began.

"Before 1972, paleontologists held to the traditional view of gradual transitions even though they hadn't found the fossils to back it up. Stephen Jay Gould and Niles Eldredge, both firm believers in evolution, stepped up to the plate and proposed the theory you have all now read about." Derek looked around to see if anyone looked guilty.

"'If evolution is true, where are the transitional fossils?' was the question Gould and Eldredge set out to answer. They proposed that there probably had never been many, because of where evolution had occurred, and because of the relatively quick pace at which it had occurred.

"The lack of fossils indicated that evolution hadn't happened among the general population as Darwin had thought, but only in something they called 'peripheral isolates.' These were on the fringes of the main population, and became the small laboratories where punctuations of evolution transpired. In these environments, natural selection did a fast work, and when a new species emerged it would quickly spread to the main population.

"Because of how few animals are actually fossilized and how comparatively quickly natural selection had worked in these isolated laboratories, we wouldn't expect to find many of the transitional forms, but only those who were so fully adapted that they spread to the main population. The fossil record today, therefore, is exactly what punctuated equilibrium would predict."

Derek was about to go on when he noticed a hand up in the back. He had called this a "lecture/discussion." "Yes?"

"It sounds to me like the emperor with no clothes," a young man who often participated in discussions stated with a puzzled frown.

"Would you care to explain that comment, Carter?" Derek wanted an atmosphere where students could open up and talk, so he tried not to sound intimidating.

"Darwin proposes a theory," the young man began, "and says we should be able to find transitional fossils if the theory is true. We don't find the fossils, but we like the theory, so we make up a new theory that doesn't demand any fossils. Now no one can question the theory without being scoffed at, even though it isn't clothed, if you will, with supporting evidence."

The problems with macroevolution seemed to be a theme in Derek's life at the moment. He decided to join Carter in his argument to see how the other students would respond.

"So what if macroevolution isn't true?" he asked. "What if the creationists are right and Darwin's theory overreached because of his anger against any god that would let his daughter die? What if only microevolution is science and macroevolution is more about faith in a system that excludes the need for a supernatural being?" Derek could not believe the questions coming out of his own mouth. It was scandalous. There was stunned silence in the class. No one knew what to say because talking about God had been taboo in all science classes up to this point. Finally one young lady ventured to speak.

"Professor Barnhouse, are you suggesting that the facts don't support macroevolution? I was brought up in a Bible believing home but have always felt that to participate in the scientific community I would have to separate my beliefs from my mind."

"Well, Natalie," Derek began, checking her name on his roster, I'd say it's still pretty safe to leave faith in God at the door in a scientific setting, because His or Her existence can't be proven. But as honest scientists, we also have to be careful to leave our scientific beliefs outside if they can't be proven or at least tested. We also have to be careful to get facts first, then make conclusions and not the other way around. Fundamentalists, for example, start with the conviction that the Bible is literally true and the earth must therefore be six thousand years old. Now they're in a jam: They can only find evidence to support that or their whole faith comes into question. Do you see why it's a bit difficult for them to find any evidence of an old earth?

"But Carter presents an interesting point. Isn't it possible that scientists have done the same thing with macroevolution? They believe the theory is true before looking at the evidence which makes it impossible to find any facts that contradict their assumption."

Derek was on a roll, almost convincing himself. The class caught his fire and hands went up everywhere. Derek let the discussion go on for another forty-five minutes. It didn't feel choked or pressured like it usually did; everyone could share whatever they wanted to with no risk of being belittled. It felt like true, honest discourse instead of a rigid acceptance of the "scientific" norm. He felt alive, and it seemed to him that his students were breathing the free air as well. He now had more questions than answers and it felt refreshingly honest.

His lawyer, Parker Vanderbilt, was waiting for him after

class.

"Are you going to treat me to lunch before our meeting?"

"What? I pay for your lunch while I pay your hourly rate? That doesn't seem right."

"That's funny, because it seems perfectly reasonable to me," Vanderbilt replied with a grin. "You're a millionaire, and I'm a lowly lawyer."

"Come on, then. But we're getting the special."

During a lunch of sushi on State Street, Derek brought his lawyer up to date on the details of his meeting with Becker. When they arrived back at Science Hall an intern escorted them into Becker's office, Radcliffe was already seated.

"Nice to see you again, Derek." He was smiling.

"Radcliffe," Derek nodded in a strained acknowledgement. "This is my lawyer, Parker Vanderbilt." Vanderbilt made quick work of the hand shaking and he and Derek sat down.

"Well, let's get right to it, gentlemen," Becker began. "I've come to an agreement with Dr. Radcliffe, and all we need is Dr. Barnhouse's signature and this unpleasant business will be behind us.

"Dr. Radcliffe will sign a waiver agreeing to never bring this subject up again. Dr. Barnhouse will sign a waiver agreeing to never expose Dr. Radcliffe's indiscretions in graduate school, write him a check immediately in the amount of $250,000, and sign over all book royalties from this time forward. I've set up an unlisted, untraceable account overseas to which the royalties will be sent, and only Dr. Radcliffe will have access to that account."

Vanderbilt looked shocked. "This is ridiculous. In a court, Radcliffe would not get a penny."

"That's neither here nor there," Becker responded. "We're not in a court of law Mr. Vanderbilt; we're in the court of public opinion. If this gets out, Dr. Barnhouse's reputation will be irrevocably tarnished by the publicity and so will the good name of this university. That's not going to happen on my watch."

"Don't we get a chance to counteroffer?" Derek felt like he had to do something, but even as he asked, he realized it was hopeless.

"Sorry, no. But if you do everything you're told you'll get to keep your place as a leading paleontolgist in this country." Derek briefly wondered how much say Mr. Becker had at home.

As Derek pulled out his checkbook he addressed Radcliffe. "Before I give this to you I have to know two things: How did you know where to dig in Comoros? And, how did an African farmer manage to contact you?"

Radcliffe smiled. "Did I never mention my Aunt Peggy to you? She established a mission in Moroni, Comoros twenty five years ago and her house is within ten miles of Mount Karthala. One of the female research assistants from the Harvard team visited the mission and went to coffee with her. The research assistant was so excited about what they were on to, she actually took Peggy out to the site while expressing regret that they couldn't stay longer. Aunty immediately e-mailed me."

"And the African farmer?" Derek questioned.

"Kintu and his family are among the few involved regularly at my aunt's mission," Radcliffe replied. "She felt she needed to tell me about Kintu's tragic cancer and his surprising confession."

"Does she know you're using his testimony to blackmail me?"

Radcliffe chuckled. "I think blackmail is too harsh, Derek. You and I are simply coming to an agreement. And why should she be soiled by the dealings of this world? I am considering sending a donation down to her though. I think she's earned it."

"She certainly has," Derek conceded as he began to write the check.

After he gave Becker the check, and signed the royalties over, he gave the nod for Vanderbilt to verify his signature with a notary stamp. When Radcliffe received the check and witnessed the signatures, Becker brought out the two waivers which both parties quickly signed. Derek and Vanderbilt left without uttering another word, both a bit stunned by the suddenness and severity of the transaction.

"Come in, it's open." Derek was back in his office and had just poured himself a healthy glass of scotch well concealed in a coffee mug with a lid.

Marie popped her head in. "I hate to disturb you. If you're busy it could wait until Monday."

"You're not disturbing me, come on in." He felt like he could use a little company right now.

"Would you like something to drink?"

"No thanks," she paused. "I came in to thank you again for giving me this job. I love the work and I think I'm going to get along fine with your team."

"You are more than welcome."

"Are you okay" she asked looking concerned. "You look a little worn out."

"The truth is I've been under a lot of stress lately. Thank you for asking."

"Do you want to talk about it?"

Yes, he really did. He couldn't tell her about Radcliffe, but he decided to share Rachel's struggle with her. Maybe she could help.

"My daughter is a senior, at the top of her class, and a beautiful young lady, but she's been sinking into depression. After questioning her a little I found that it's mainly about the randomness of evolution. She wants to believe that there is more than natural selection guiding this planet. She wishes there was an after-life."

"What did you tell her?"

"That it takes courage to face the facts and that she is a courageous young lady for facing these tough questions so young. I don't think it did much for her."

Marie's eyes were shining now. "I bet it meant the world to have her dad so proud of her. I wouldn't worry, she's probably just going through a stage."

"What bothers me the most, Marie, is the thing she is depressed about has been my life's message. Is it possible that my message is wrong, and I've been leading her down the wrong path?"

"How could it be wrong when all you've ever done is teach what science has taught you?" Marie countered.

"Well, I'm wondering whether it all really was science. Does science alone contain the answers for life? What if there really is more than the material realm? What if there is a God who created everything? What if there is a purpose for human beings, and what if there really is an after-life we should be preparing for?" Derek knew he was letting the scotch get to him to ask these questions in front of an assistant.

Marie looked a bit bewildered. She reached over and gently patted his hand. "I think you've had a long week and just need a good night's sleep. Rachel has been trained by the best and will do great; she just needs to get her feet under her."

She smiled as she got up to go. "I need to get back to my mom. She's kind of a control freak and wants me to be back exactly when she expects me. You understand, I'm sure."

"Of course. Thanks for listening, Marie. Say 'hi' to your mom for me and tell her she has a very wise daughter." As he added a wink, he was shocked at his audacity. He was flirting with a student! Or, practically a student, anyway.

Marie smiled and winked slowly back at him with a twinkle in her eye.

"I'll see you tomorrow." She put her hand on the door

knob. "Good night, Derek."

Derek felt his face flush. He couldn't believe he was affected so much. It just wasn't right. He finished his scotch and determined that he would be more professional around Marie in the future.

"Does anyone want to watch Braveheart with me?" Derek asked that night after a light supper of BLTs, salad, and chips.

"Braveheart?" Theresa faked a gag. "Too much violence. Isn't there something a little less serious?"

"I don't know why, but that's what I'm in the mood for. I could watch it in our bedroom."

"Oh, I don't care what you watch. I'll be reading my book anyway."

"I'd love to, Dad," Jared said. "But we're having a little scrimmage tonight to get ready for tomorrow's game. You coming?"

"To the all-star game? I wouldn't miss it."

"I'll watch with you," Rachel offered. "I've got nothing else going on, and it sure beats trying to figure out my existence."

Derek made the popcorn and sat in his favorite chair while Rachel lay on the couch under a comforter with a pillow under her head. Derek manned the remote control to their wide screen television.

"Are you ready?" he asked as he pressed play.

After watching a three hour movie in almost complete silence, Derek and Rachel both still had tears in their eyes when the credits finished, and the set was turned off.

"Do you think there are things more important than survival?" Rachel asked.

Derek thought a minute before responding. "I think so. Maybe I didn't, but I'm rethinking a lot of things I just assumed were true in the past."

"Do you think you've really lived?"

"What do you mean?"

"You know, when Wallace says, 'All men die, but few men really live.' Do you just feel like you're existing or do you feel like you're fully living?"

Derek had never told Rachel about his dreams or his "fully alive" thoughts. He found it interesting that she used a similar phrase.

"To be honest, Rach, I think I've touched fully alive, but I don't live there. I don't know if anyone does."

Rachel fell silent and Derek was grateful. He wasn't ready to share the dreams with her because he still didn't know what it all meant.

CHAPTER 9

S aturday was Jared's all-star basketball game at Madison West High School, and for a change, Derek was able to attend. As a 6'3" junior forward, Jared had made first team in the conference. He wasn't that tall, but the boy had springs in his legs, and a fade away that 6'10" centers had a hard time blocking.

Theresa sat on one side, while his daughter, who had to be dragged along, sat on the other. His kids were very different from each other. Whereas Rachel thought deeply, Jared tended to skim the surface. Rachel poured herself into her studies, while Jared poured himself into sports, especially basketball. And he was a delight to watch.

The Triple A all-star game featured the best high school players in the state. The eastern stars were mainly from the Milwaukee area, and the west from Madison, but there were a few from schools as far away as Green Bay on the east, and LaCrosse on the west.

Jared's team handled the tip and were off and running. A guard from LaFollette hit Jared with a bounce pass that led to a reverse layup and the first points of the game. The fans were on their feet cheering as loudly as they could.

It was a close game. The East had a 6'5" guard who caught fire from three point range or the West may have run away with it early. By half time it was East - 40 and West - 39. When the teams came back out, Derek, Theresa, and even Rachel were on their feet with all the other fans going crazy.

The West scored the first six points of the third period, but the East came right back with four of their own. It kept going back and forth until about halfway through the third period when Jared had a breakaway to take the lead. As he was going in for a stuff, the 6'5" kid from East ran into him full tilt while attempting to make a block. When Jared came down his leg twisted under him with the East player on top of him. He gave out a blood curdling scream of pain. The gymnasium was stunned into a shocked silence as they watched him writhe on the floor.

Derek shot up and ran to the floor with Theresa and Rachel behind him, reaching Jared at the same time the coach did.

"What is it, Son?" The coach asked.

"It's my knee, I heard it snap."

The coach turned to his assistant and told him to call for the ambulance. Jared looked at Derek with tears in his eyes.

"It's really bad. I can't move it at all. Do you think this is it for my career, Dad?"

Derek got on a knee and took his hand. "It's amazing what they can do today, Buddy. They'll sew you up, do a little physical therapy, and no one will ever know it happened." He was struggling to be positive because he had heard the snap all the way from his seat.

"I hope you're right." He glanced over Derek's shoulder. "Hey Mom, Rach. Sorry you had to see this."

Derek watched the paramedics put his son on a stretcher. It didn't seem real. This can't be happening. Jared and the ambulance crew seemed to fade and shrink into the distance, as memory after memory flooded Derek's mind. Jared's first basketball. The little guy could hardly hold it. Hours together out in the driveway, shooting hoops, passing, blocking, practicing lay ups. His first game. The time the team came from being behind 32 points and winning in overtime. The first time Derek couldn't make a game. The times Jared begged him to shoot some hoops with him. The day he stopped begging. The times Derek tried to explain that his job required him to travel. "But, Dad, who is more important to you, me or these college students halfway around the world?" Jared couldn't understand Derek's reply, and now Derek wasn't sure he understood it himself.

They had drifted apart. Maybe that was why Jared was suddenly too busy to be with Derek. Maybe that was why Jared always made a joke out of everything. The only serious thing in Jared's life was basketball.

And now this.

The rest of the day was spent in the hospital because the doctors decided to operate immediately when they saw the extent of the damage. By ten o'clock they were back home with Jared on crutches, struggling to not be depressed.

"Do you think it's possible we're in the middle of a spiritual conflict?" Derek asked when he and Theresa were alone in the bedroom.

"What are you talking about?"

"Let me tell you about a second dream I had," Derek began. "It started kind of where the first dream ended, with this guy looking at me real close and a warm sensation going through me. But then his eyes changed to fiery anger and his gaze lifted above me. When I turned to see what he was looking at I was horrified at the sight of a large, black, gargoyle type being right over my shoulder. I was trembling when I woke up. It was so real that I can still see every detail clearly if I want to.

"When I asked Brian about it, he said that he thought there was a spiritual conflict between light and darkness with me in the middle. And that's exactly how I feel."

"Just because of a basketball injury?" Theresa questioned, "I don't get it."

"There's more going on than that, Theresa, and I'm sorry I didn't tell you about it earlier, but I didn't want you to worry."

"About what?"

Derek then recalled the demand by Radcliffe, and the eventual settlement in complete detail. Theresa was furious.

"You didn't want to worry me, so you paid a bribe of a quarter million dollars without consulting me?" Theresa was boiling over. "Do you think I'm a child, Derek? I'm your wife and a full grown adult with a law degree! You don't have to protect me from the real world!"

"I just didn't feel like there was anything anyone could do. I'm sorry."

"At least let me be part of the process of deciding there's nothing that can be done. It's not the money I'm worried about, it's our marriage. Good night!"

Sometimes Theresa was just done talking. Derek knew that it was best to just leave it and give her space until she worked it through.

CHAPTER 10

It was Sunday morning and Derek was up early making coffee when Rachel came downstairs.

"Hey, what are you doing up so early?" he asked her.

"I promised a friend a long time ago that I would go to a service at City Church with her. It's a Bible church that has modern music, and she has been asking me to go for about two years. I told her I'd go if she would stop bugging me and let me choose the time."

"And today's the day?"

"Yeah, why not. I thought if we went to the early service I'd still have lots of time to hang out and relax."

As Derek took a cup of coffee down to his study he found it funny that his daughter was going to church, and he was studying Genesis. What's wrong with this picture? It had occurred to him at some point that he didn't need a Bible; he could just google Genesis and read right off the computer screen.

"In the beginning God created the heavens and the earth. And the earth was without form, and void; and darkness was over the surface of the deep; and the Spirit of God was moving over the surface of the waters... " is how it began.

Derek read the first two chapters of Genesis three straight times as they seemed to be the complementary chapters that covered creation. The third time through he decided to keep going. In chapter three he was surprised at the presence of an evil serpent in a world that God had declared "very good." There was no explanation of where he came from. He read about the fall and God's judgment as well as His promise of a future time when the serpent's head would be crushed.

Man's selfishness never surprised Derek, it was part of surviving, but the added dimension of God's active intervention was very interesting. He read about the ark and the flood; he read about the tower of Babel; and then about Abraham, Isaac, and Jacob. It was amazing how many literary references there were to these stories, and yet somehow, he had never been required to read them. As he was reading about Jacob's wrestling match with an angel there was a light tap at the door.

"Good morning, can I come in?" It was Theresa.

"Good morning, and how did you sleep?"

"It started bad, but got better after I forgave you. Not that you deserved it, but I needed to get some rest, so I let go of it." She smiled at him as she took a drink from her coffee.

"Well, whatever the motive, I'm glad to be back on good terms."

"Did I say good? My not being mad anymore doesn't necessarily mean good. It just means it could be good, so be on your best behavior." She was kind of kidding and that was a promising sign.

"Derek, what are you going to do about Jared?"

Derek looked up. "What about Jared?"

"His friends are on their way to the mall and he wants to go with them. He's loaded up on pain killers, and I thought the doctor made it clear that the leg should be kept up as much as possible. But he won't listen to me."

Derek grimaced. "I don't think he'll listen to me either, T. He's seventeen so I think he needs to be the one to decide. He'll be the one who will suffer later."

"Oh, I guess you're right," Theresa sighed with frustration and then moved closer to the computer. "What are you reading?"

"Genesis. It's an assignment Brian gave me before I meet with Dr. Charles Crowder while I'm in Chicago tomorrow."

"Since when does anyone give you an assignment?" she asked in an astonished tone of voice.

"I like Brian and he really wanted me to meet this old Hebrew professor who believes the Bible can be interpreted to allow for an old earth, and I want to hear what he says. Brian said that Dr. Crowder would also like to hear my dreams."

"Brian, Brian. What, you've known him for two weeks and now it sounds like he's one of your best friends."

"Are you jealous that I have a new friend?" he laughed.

"It's not that. It's just that he's not your normal type of friend. This guy seems to be into the Bible and praying. Have you ever hung out with anyone like that before?"

"Can't a guy step out of his routine and try something new once in awhile? I'm stretching myself."

"Whatever," she shrugged. "If you want breakfast or lunch at some point, find me and we can eat together like a husband and wife should."

Just then they heard Jared yelling "bye" on his way out.

Theresa just shook her head. After a sip of her coffee she asked, "by the way, where's Rachel?"

"Oh, she went to church." At that Theresa excused herself with a look of bewilderment.

As Derek finished Genesis with the story of Joseph in Genesis, chapter fifty, Rachel came in with a big smile on her face.

"Hey girl, what's up? You look happy."

"I liked church, Dad."

"What do you mean you liked it?"

"The singing was intense and near the end I felt something warm inside me, like I was being wrapped up in peace." Now she really had Derek's attention. "The sermon was about a guy named Elijah and how he went through a time of depression. The preacher called it the 'cave of discouragement.' He said God will never send you to that cave, but He will always follow if you end up in it. He described exactly how I've been feeling. It makes me wonder if God is real and is trying to get my attention. He's sure real to those people."

Derek was starting to feel the warmth from his dream right there in his study. "Do you want to hear about the dreams I've had recently, Rachel?"

"Dreams? Like what kind of dreams?"

"Come and ride with me, I'll tell you in the car. I need to buy a Bible before tomorrow and you can help me."

Derek told every detail of his dreams, about his talks with Brian, and even had her read the passage out of the Gideon's Testament about Jesus. They were headed east on the beltline for University Bookstore. By the time they arrived, Rachel was so excited about what he had shared that she wanted a Bible too.

"Dad, this is a little overwhelming," Rachel commented as she viewed all the different translations and types of Bibles. "How do we choose?"

"Well, it needs to be the New International Version because that's the one Dr. Crowder worked on. And it should probably be one with marginal notes, since we really don't know anything yet."

After they both chose a Bible they headed home and continued to talk about the spiritual adventure they seemed to be on. Derek couldn't remember a time he felt closer to his daughter.

"How about I cook on the grill for us tonight?" Derek suggested early that evening as he came up behind Theresa and gave her a back rub.

"Sounds great, what are you making?"

"Barbequed ribs with baked potatoes and Caesar salad?" He was asking, not announcing, because he wanted it to be something she would enjoy.

"Yum. What should I do?"

"Your only job is to drink lemonade by the pool and read your book."

"I'll see if I can summon the strength. Hey, are you just trying to get on my good side?"

"What if I am?"

"It's starting to work, keep it up."

She gave him a little kiss, and retreated out of the kitchen quickly, as if he might change his mind.

A car door slammed outside, so Derek knew that Jared was home.

"What's for dinner? I'm starved," Jared announced as he hobbled in on his crutches.

"Well, I'm glad to see that your knee hasn't affected your stomach. How does it feel now?"

"Very sore. Mom was right. It didn't help ambling around the mall all afternoon. After I assured Katy that our prom date is still on, she continued the search for a dress, and I think she tried on every possibility in the entire place just to see what I thought." Katy was a good friend who Jared had asked to next Saturday's prom.

"Did she find one?"

"No. Apparently that isn't the point. First, you have to shop around to know what's out there. The actual purchase is a whole separate trip."

Derek laughed. "Well, at least you've worked up an appetite. How do barbequed ribs on the grill sound?"

"Bring it on!" was Jared's brief, but excited reply.

"Are you still worried about Radcliffe leaking your secret out?" Theresa asked later that night when they were getting ready for bed.

"Not really. He looked pretty happy about the settlement. Things probably worked out in his best interests for me to find micropteryx instead of him, and I think he realizes it."

"Where did you take a quarter million dollars from?"

"I sold some stock and cashed in an annuity with a small penalty for early withdrawal. We'll be alright."

"I sure hope you know what you're doing, because I don't think I would have agreed, IF you had included me in the decision."

"Are you going to have to forgive me again to get some sleep?"

"Sometimes I forgive but have trouble forgetting. Don't let it happen again, pal." She was playful, but serious.

"I won't. Do you mind if I read a little?"

"Suit yourself. Just make sure the light is off when you go to sleep," Theresa requested as she rolled over.

Derek began Exodus, the second book of the Bible. He read the first nineteen chapters without stopping but Exodus 20:11 surprised him so much he couldn't get past it. God was comparing creation to the six day work week when he said, "For in six days the Lord made the heavens and the earth, the sea, and all that is in them, but he rested on the seventh day."

His original thought about Genesis chapter one was that they were 24 hour days because of the language, "there was evening and there was morning," which seemed to imply a solar day. But then it occurred to him that the sun wasn't even made until day four, so maybe the days weren't solar, but God sized days where each day represented an entire age of creation. He had felt certain this was the argument Dr. Crowder would make from the passage, allowing for an old earth.

But this verse was clearly about a week with seven days. God created everything in six days and rested on the seventh.

If Adam was made on day six, the sun and the earth would only be a few days younger. If that were the case, the Bible really did teach that the earth was only six thousand years old. His mind was spinning, so he decided it was time for bed. He would ask Dr. Crowder about it tomorrow.

CHAPTER 11

Monday morning Derek picked up Marie at her house for their trip to Chicago. They worked in the car planning the next dig and reviewing all the information he was going to need for a speech next week in New York. Marie was a little nervous because her mom wasn't doing well but had insisted on coming anyway even though Derek offered her the day off. She would run his book table for both the morning and evening lecture as well as screen the people who wanted to see him. He couldn't meet with everyone but didn't mind answering a few questions and signing a few autographs.

After the first lecture they had lunch with the geology staff at Northwestern and then retreated back to the Holiday Inn where they were staying for the afternoon. They were planning to drive back to Madison late that night.

Derek had just laid down for a quick nap when there was a tap at the door. When he opened it, he found Marie standing in the doorway with tears streaming down her face.

"Marie, please come in," he gently prodded, "tell me what's wrong."

"My Dad just called. Mom died twenty minutes ago," she managed to get out through a fresh stream of tears.

"I am truly sorry," Derek said as he embraced her.

Marie cried on his shoulder and held on tight like she

would never let go. Derek could feel her firm, yet well rounded body against him. He was stroking her hair in a comforting way and smelling the aroma of her perfume when he kissed the top of her head. She raised her face slightly, and he kissed her again on the forehead. Then she looked him in the eyes and slowly pulled his head down giving him a gentle kiss on the lips. Electricity was flowing through him.

He then kissed her and she responded. When he kissed her again they both gave way to a passion that they had been holding back since they first met. His hands were starting to go up the back of her blouse when he heard a "no" inside of him. He tried to ignore it, but it kept getting louder until he finally pulled away from the embrace.

Marie looked bewildered. "What's wrong?"

"This is wrong, and I'm very sorry. I'm your employer which is bad enough; I'm also happily married which makes it worse; and to top it off, you are vulnerable because you're grieving. Please forgive me, Marie."

Marie went cold. "The last I knew I was a consenting adult."

She gathered her thoughts before speaking again. "I want this, Derek, and you do too."

"I'm so sorry, Marie, but I really don't." He felt like he needed to be firm and give no thought of a future romance. Now that the electricity was gone, something had changed. She seemed more like a daughter than a lover.

"If you want to take the car back now, I'd be happy to fly later?" he offered.

She suddenly looked as hard as nails. "I already have a taxi taking me to the airport in a half hour. Goodbye, Dr. Barnhouse," she said in an abrupt tone as she turned to leave.

"Marie, please charge all of your expenses to my department, I insist," Derek urged, but he wasn't sure it did any good. She was gone. *Hell hath no fury like a woman scorned* was what he thought to himself as he was left standing alone.

Dr. Charles Crowder lived in Palos Heights, Chicago, and Derek pulled into the driveway right on schedule Monday afternoon thanks to Mapquest. The Crowders had a one car garage attached to their small, but well kept up split-level home.

"And you must be Derek," a gray haired woman opened the door with a big smile on her face. "I'm Myrtle," she said, as she shook his hand. "Come right in."

"You're right on time young man, I like that. I'm Charles." Charles Crowder was 86 years old and was wearing a red cardigan over a dress shirt that looked like it had gone out of style about 40 years ago. There was an unmistakable warmth about him combined with a sharpness of intellect that made Derek want to know him.

"Come on down to my study," Charles encouraged after some small talk with coffee.

The study smelled like a combination of old books, pipe tobacco, and well used leather. The small lamp on his desk was still on, highlighting open books and study materials that gave the impression Dr. Crowder was anything but retired.

"Now sit down, Derek, and start by telling me your dreams."

It took a half hour to get through this because Charles had questions about everything. He wanted details of what the eyes looked like, and what the warmth felt like, and how the gargoyle had trembled. He then lit up his pipe and just sat quiet; deep in thought. Finally, he spoke again.

"I'm convinced young man that you have seen our Lord as well as an angel of darkness, possibly Satan himself. Are you aware of how the Lord spoke to His children and even those who weren't yet His children, throughout the scriptures?"

"Ahhh, I'd never even read much of the Bible until this weekend," Derek answered hesitantly. "Sunday, I read about

Jacob's dream when he slept on a stone; and Joseph's dreams about future greatness; and then Pharoah's dreams that caused Joseph's release from prison. But that's about it."

"You have given the start of a pattern we find throughout the scripture," Dr. Crowder began. "Many years after Pharoah, God gave another king, named Nebuchadnezzer, a dream when the children of Israel were held captive in Babylon. No one could interpret it because he wouldn't even reveal what the dream was. Then God gave Daniel the exact same dream, with the interpretation, and eventually Nebuchadnezzer came to faith in the Lord. Daniel had many other dreams that told about the kingdoms that would follow Babylon, and about the end times.

"In the New Testament Joseph received a dream telling him to not be afraid to wed Mary, the mother of our Lord. Later, he received another dream telling him to leave for Egypt, and when he was in Egypt, another was given, telling him to go back. The apostle Paul had a dream telling him to go to Macedonia, and another time the Lord Himself appeared to him in a vision of the night, telling him to keep preaching in Corinth.

"Job 33:14-17 says God uses dreams sometimes to get through to people that aren't listening to anything else."

"What's it say?" Derek asked.

Professor Crowder began to recite from memory, "Indeed God speaks once, or twice, yet no one notices it. In a dream, a vision of the night, when sound sleep falls on men while they slumber in their beds, then He opens the ears of men, and seals their instruction, that He may turn man aside from his conduct, and keep man from pride."

"Wow, that's pretty straight forward.*" Was it possible that the Bible really was inspired by God?* Derek wondered. His mind was reeling from the possibility.

"You've been given a great privilege."

Dr. Crowder paused and then spoke again, "But this isn't

why you came, you wanted to hear about my interpretation of the Bible that allows for an old earth."

"I think it's great that you're modern enough to reinterpret the Bible to accomodate what scientists have found to be true," Derek said sincerely, thinking he was giving a compliment.

"You have me all wrong, young man. We don't look at science and then try to get the Bible to match it. The Bible stands as the unaltered Word of God forever established in the heavens. Once in awhile it seems that the Bible and science contradict one another, but science eventually catches up, given enough time.

"Scientists used to think the world was flat, but Isaiah had said all along that God sits upon the circle of the earth. Scientists used to believe that there were only 7,000 stars when God had told Abraham that the stars were innumerable, like the sand in the sea. Scientists used to believe the earth was eternal until the early 1900s when they agreed it must have had a beginning, just like the Bible had said all along. Evolution today maintains that one species arose from another, but honest scientists will eventually come to the truth that he made 'each after its own kind.'

"When I met with the original committee here in Palos Heights in 1965, the last thing we were worried about was what scientists now believed. We met to talk about the need for a translation of the Bible in modern day English that could take advantage of the ancient texts discovered in the Dead Sea scrolls. We split up the translation among committees that included over one hundred Hebrew and Greek scholars from every denomination of Christianity. I happened to be part of the group responsible for translating Genesis.

"There are only about 20,000 Hebrew words today, Derek, and in the ancient language, about half that. What that means is that the same Hebrew word is often used in many different ways. Only the context decides which interpretation is correct." Dr. Crowder rose and motioned for Derek to follow as he slipped behind his desk motioning for Derek to sit across from him.

"When it came to translating 'hayah' in Genesis 1:2 I felt strongly that in its context it should be translated 'became' instead of 'was'." He flipped the monitor around so Derek could read the passage.

"And the earth was without form, and void; and darkness was upon the face of the deep. And the spirit of God moved upon the face of the water," is what it read.

"I couldn't convince my peers completely, because no other translation had used 'became', but they did agree on an asterisk next to 'was' with a note at the bottom that says, 'or possibly became.'(12) It is the first footnote in the NIV Bible."

"I don't understand. Why would 'became' instead of 'was' in one verse allow for an old earth?" Derek asked.

Dr. Crowder hesitated before answering. Derek could tell that he was trying to make it as simple as possible for him to understand.

"Genesis 1:1 says that 'In the beginning God created the heavens and the earth.' Verse two says, 'And the earth was without form, and void.' If it were to read, 'And the earth became without form, and void,' it would mean that something happened to the original creation that made the earth become 'without form, and void.'"

"Why do you think something happened? The Bible seems to be a pretty straight forward book to not mention it."

"Yes, it does, until you get to Genesis 3:1 and find a serpent that is already evil in a world that God called 'very good.'"

"Yeah, I noticed that," Derek was excited. "Where did he come from?"

Dr. Crowder was now clearly in his element. "Jesus said that 'Satan was a murderer from the beginning' in John 8:44. From whose beginning? If it was his own beginning then you would have to believe that God created evil which is unthinkable. It can only mean from our beginning, the beginning of this creation. Everything God made in those six days was 'very good,' but there was someone left over, apparently from a past creation. Consider this scriptural evidence of a previous creation that was destroyed by a flood:

First, "without form and void" are translations of the Hebrew words: 'Tohu va Bohu.' The phrase 'tohu va bohu' is used only two other times in all of scripture. Once in Isaiah 34:8-10 where God is describing a devastating judgment that is coming on Edom; and once in Jeremiah 4:22-23 where He is describing desolating judgment that will come on Israelites who have been in rebellion. If two of the three places describe terrible judgment, isn't it logical that the third use is the same?"

Secondly, Ezekiel 28 describes Satan before his fall as being beautiful, perfect in all his ways, and an anointed cherub that was in an Eden where every precious stone was his covering. He was on earth, but not our current earth. This was an earth that was destroyed by a flood in reponse to Satan's rebellion against God. That's why we find the earth under water in verse two. His rebellion is more fully described in Isaiah 14 which identifies Satan's given name as Lucifer, or Morning Star. From the beginning of this creation he was already a murderer, that's why he is already evil in Genesis 3.

Thirdly, in Genesis 1:9-10 God gathers the waters together and dry land appears. He calls the dry land, 'earth.' God's own definition of earth is 'dry land,' not land that's covered with water. Doesn't it make sense that the 'earth' He created in verse one was dry land? And that the dry land was later flooded by water, so that by verse two we find the Spirit brooding over the waters of an earth that had become without form and void.

And finally, in Isaiah 45:18 the Bible says that God "did not create (the earth) in a waste place (tohu), but to be inhabited." If God didn't create the earth 'tohu,' then it must have become 'tohu' sometime after He made it."

Derek was impressed by Dr. Crowder's reasoning but he knew he had to ask his question.

"Dr. Crowder, doesn't it say in Exodus 20:11 that God made the heavens and the earth and the sea in six days and rested on the seventh? It sounds to me like everything happened in 144 hours."

The doctor laughed. "My, you've done quite a bit of reading in one weekend, haven't you? That is a great question, Derek, and actually a proof text used by young earth creationists.

Dr. Crowder now went into a detailed explanation of the different Hebrew words used for 'create' and 'made'. He showed how the heaven and earth God "created" in verse one were different than the heaven and earth He "made" in verses seven through ten. The heaven and earth in verse one were created out of nothing before the seven days even began, while the heaven and earth He made during days two and three were both out of preexisting materials. Exodus 20:11, he argued, used the word "made" and not "create" because it is referring only to what God made during the six days. (See appendix for full explanation)

After twenty minutes of this, Derek was convinced and really needed to get going to be on time for his lecture.

"Thank you, Dr. Crowder. I am now confident that it is possible to reconcile the Bible with an old earth. It might interest you that geologists have identified at least two major catastrophes in our past: one is called the Permian extinction and the other is called the 'K-T' extinction at the end of the Cretaceous era, which they believe exterminated the dinosaurs and a great deal more besides.(13) It seems the Bible points to at least two catastrophes as well: the flood destroying Satan's kingdom, and the flood in the days of Noah."

"That's interesting, Derek," he said, but seemed to be contemplating something else. "Before you go could I give you one last encouragement?"

"Certainly."

"The reason why our team worked together so well in the late 60s was that we distinguished between the essentials and non-essentials in Christianity. On central truths like the authority of the Bible; the fact that God created for a purpose; and that salvation is through Christ alone; we were in complete agreement.

"But on other things such as the age of the earth, how to baptize, and what will be the order of end times events, we differed. We allowed differences in non-essentials as long as there was unity in the essentials. However you end up interpreting Genesis, I hope that you will remember that it's not worth dividing Christians to prove your point."

"I will try to remember, thank you Doctor." Derek shook his hand. "And thanks again for taking the time to meet with me. You don't know how much this means."

"The pleasure was all mine, son. Thank you for sharing your dreams and know that Myrtle and I will be praying for you."

Derek said goodbye and then rushed back to the campus to do the evening lecture. It was a good thing he could give this speech in his sleep because he wasn't sure what he believed anymore.

CHAPTER 12

After a late night of driving and about five hours of sleep, Derek was back at the office drinking his morning coffee while staring at a handwritten note from Marilyn Becker:

Derek,

> There have been some disturbing rumors going around like wild fire related to what you're teaching. We need to meet this morning before your first lecture. See you at 9:00 in my office.

Becker

Rumors? What could this possibly be? Oh well, he would go and ease the Dean's fears that something was amiss on her watch. When Derek arrived he was disturbed by the presence of Everett Stone in the office with Dr. Becker.

"Why is he here?" Derek started.

"Dr. Stone has heard some rumors from his students and I wanted him to bring them directly to you," Becker explained.

"So, why didn't he?"

"Well, that's what he's doing now."

"No, he came to you, not me, or you wouldn't be here. What goes on in this university is childish. Stone tattles on me because of a rumor he heard, so I have to meet with mom to be scolded. It's ridiculous."

"Dr. Barnhouse, I'll have you know that the accusations which have been made are not ridiculous but gravely serious. I'm sure if they were less so, Dr. Stone would have gone to you first. Everett, tell us what has been going around."

"Did you, or did you not," Stone began like a prosecuting attorney, "question, in front of your students, the truth of macroevolution?"

"Yes, I did. So what?" Derek wasn't going to back down.

"Did you, or did you not, compare modern day evolutionists to young earth creationists who put their beliefs before the facts?"

"More or less, so what?"

Stone went on with an air of condescension. "Maybe you didn't realize this, Dr. Barnhouse, but we are in a cultural war in this country between science and fundamentalism. We must present a united front or we fuel religious fanaticism."

"I maintained in the same lecture that I believe the facts point to an old earth. Did anyone mention that in the rumor mill?"

"No, they didn't," Stone replied. "Why? Is that supposed to comfort us? We are evolutionists at this university, Barnhouse. If you aren't one anymore there is no place for you here."

Everett Stone's eyes were bulging, kind of like the gargoyle in his dream. Although there was only pride and anger in his voice, he could see fear in his eyes. He wasn't sure why.

"I am a scientist first, Dr. Stone," Derek said in a calm, steady voice. "I am a tenured professor at this university and work here to train up scientific minds. I believe in the fact of microevolution because it has been proven. I am asking difficult questions about macroevolution which I thought was the nature of scientific inquiry."

Both Becker and Stone seemed frustrated by him. The argument was over. Becker spoke with authority now.

"Dr. Barnhouse, because of the proliferation of these rumors Dr. Stone has requested a meeting for all the faculty in our department, and I have approved. It is scheduled for 10:00 o'clock on Thursday morning, but it doesn't need to be a lengthy meeting. I will ask you three questions, and you will answer each of them for everyone on our faculty to hear. I want these rumors stopped. Is that clear?" Becker was waiting.

"You are clear, Marilyn. What are the questions?"

Becker now looked like she was back in control as she gave each question slowly, apparently so he could understand how important they were.

"One, do you believe in an old earth? Two, do you renounce religious dogmatism that puts belief before facts? And three, do you believe in macroevolution as the explanation of how all things came to be?"

"And what if I don't give the answers you want the faculty to hear?" Derek asked.

Now Becker had the gargoyle eyes. "You will give the right answers, Dr. Barnhouse. Thursday morning, ten o'clock sharp."

The meeting was over. No more discussion and no more questions. Just those eyes daring him to cross her. Derek let go of it. There was nothing they could do to a tenured professor who had different ideas, except possibly exhort him to be more careful around the students. It wasn't as big a deal as Stone and Becker were making of it.

CHAPTER 13

After Stone left her office, Marilyn Becker was left stewing over the potential ramifications of Barnhouse not lining up when her cell phone rang.

"Hello, Marilyn Becker," she answered.

"Dean Becker, this is Chancellor Stoltenmeyer." It was troubling the Franklin Stoltenmeyer was using official titles when they were usually casual with one another.

"Chancellor Stoltenmeyer, what a surprise. And how may I help you?"

"Dean Becker, I received a call from Robert Ruperson today that is troubling me."

"Who's Robert Ruperson?" she asked.

"Ruperson is a multi-millionaire who has taken an interest in Derek Barnhouse's work. He came here last week to set up an endowment for $5,000,000 that would pay Barnhouse's salary as well as fund all digs he is part of for the next ten years. It would be a boon for the university."

"And why is that troubling?" Becker asked.

"Because the paper work isn't completed yet, and today, I talked to an unhappy Mr. Ruperson. It seems his favorite niece is in Barnhouse's class and says that he's been questioning evolution in front of the students. Do you know about this?"

"As a matter of fact rumors of this have come to me as well," Becker began. "I met with Dr. Barnhouse just this morning, and we plan on clearing up the confusion his remarks generated in a faculty department meeting on Thursday morning. In fact, because of how quickly the rumors have spread, I'm opening the meeting to faculty members university wide who have heard them and been concerned."

"Was he playing the devil's advocate or is he really questioning evolution?" the chancellor asked in a gentler tone.

"I don't know, sir." There was an uneasy silence for an awkward amount of time.

"Let me say it this way, Dean Becker." Any gentleness was gone, and now the general was giving orders: "He had better renounce any doubts he's having in front of our faculty and assure us all that he won't stir up our students again in this way. I don't need to remind you that we are an academic institution that values only scientific explanations of our universe."

"You don't need to remind me, Chancellor, and be assured, I will do everything in my power to make sure Barnhouse comes around. I will report to you promptly afterwards if you'd like."

"You won't have to report to me, Dean Becker. I will be in that meeting."

With that comment Chancellor Franklin Stoltenmeyer hung up.

As Marilyn Becker considered her options she went through her rolodex and stopped at the card of a CNN reporter who had done a special on the Madison campus last year.

"Maybe another rumor is necessary to bring the mighty Dr. Barnhouse around," she said to herself as she picked up the phone.

CHAPTER 14

Derek had just finished his last lecture of the day when his cell phone rang.

"Barnhouse."

"Derek you need to get home," Theresa was in a panic. "USA Today and CNN have called here wanting to get your response to the accusations of fraud in the finding of micropteryx. Radcliffe must have leaked and now the story is everywhere."

"Ahhhh, okay, I'll be home soon," he mumbled as he pressed end.

Derek was shell shocked. What had happened? He had been sure that Radcliffe was happy with the settlement. It just didn't make sense. Maybe Marilyn could help him track Radcliffe down, so he could get to the bottom of this. He knocked on her office door.

"Come in, it's open." She was now all sweetness and smiles.

"I've got some bad news."

"What's wrong?"

"Well, it seems that Radcliffe has leaked because USA Today and CNN have called my house giving me a chance to respond before they run their stories on what they called 'the micropteryx fraud.'" *Why doesn't she look upset?*

"I know all about it, Derek, they've called here too."

"They have? What did you tell them?"

"We told them that we will look into the accusations but didn't feel they would change anything, even if there was some truth in them. We're going to stand behind you, Derek, no matter what the world says." Becker now rose and put a hand on Derek's shoulder. "That's how we are at this university. We play as a team and we stick together."

Derek stood as well. It was becoming clear to him what was going on. "I've got to go."

He was being blackmailed. The unspoken message from Becker was, "you toe the line with our science, or we will remove you for unethical behavior that gives us ground to break your tenure." Derek felt like he was trapped in a corner with no place to go.

As he drove into his garage he couldn't help remembering his life a few weeks earlier. How could so much go wrong so quickly? He had no intention of responding to the national press. What he needed was time to think.

Rachel and Jared were both doing things with friends, so he and Theresa sat down to a meal alone. Derek immediately poured out the whole dilemma.

"So, just tell them what they want to hear," Theresa responded after hearing the story. "You probably shouldn't have voiced your doubts in front of your students, Derek. It would be like a pastor questioning his faith in God right in front of the congregation."

"I still believe in science, Theresa. And I've done nothing wrong except ask some difficult questions about macro-evolution. They haven't responded with a discussion about the facts but with threats. Aren't we supposed to be looking for the truth? Am I only supposed to think about my own survival regardless of what the facts of science say? How is that fair to the students?"

"I don't know, Honey," Theresa got up and put her arms around him. "I just know that you've been going through a lot lately, and there is a danger of you doing something hasty you'll regret later."

She seemed tender and sympathetic. Why not get the full weight of what was bothering him off his chest? "Theresa, would you mind if I told you about something else that happened at work?"

"What?"

Did he really want to tell her about Marie? Why stir the pot up unnecessarily? But hadn't she just said the other day that she was an adult with a law degree and didn't have to be shielded from the truth? Besides, he had eventually done the right thing, hadn't he?

Just then he heard the sound of a car driving up.

"It's nothing, Honey, I'm sorry I even brought it up. Hey, it looks like Rachel's here."

The door swung open, "Hi Dad, Mom."

"You sure look happy," Derek observed, "What's up?"

"Well, it just so happens that I have met some new friends, and they invited me to their Bible study on Wednesday nights."

"What kind of a group is this?"

"It's called Campus Life. A lot of kids in our school go to it for fun, but I'm going because they have a time at the end where they talk about the Bible. I want to learn as much as I can before I leave for college."

"Be careful, Rachel," Theresa warned. "We all know how much damage religious fanaticism has done in this world."

"I will, Mom. But this seems to be more about a relationship with God than about any specific religious system. Don't worry though, I'll keep my eyes open. Did I miss dinner?"

"There are leftovers in the fridge. Help yourself."

Derek was falling asleep when Theresa asked the question. "What else happened at work?"

"Nothing, really. I'm sorry I ever brought it up."

Theresa turned the table lamp on. "I want to know. What is it?"

"Marie's mom died," he said matter of factly.

"You could have told me that earlier. What else happened?" Theresa was not going to let this go.

"We were at the Holiday Inn and she knocked on my door to tell me about her mom. I invited her in and gave her a hug to make her feel better. Well, one thing led to another and we started kissing, but I stopped it and told her it was wrong."

"You did what?" Theresa was fuming. "You kiss a beautiful woman fifteen years younger than you when she has just lost her mom, and you're proud of yourself for stopping? Well, let me congratulate you." The sarcasm was so thick you could cut it.

Theresa now burst into tears. Derek didn't know what to do; she was sobbing loudly. He put a hand on her shoulder.

"Get away from me! How could you, Derek? What? I haven't been meeting your needs, so you have to look around at work? How many others have there been?"

"Theresa, you're blowing this way out of proportion! I love you and you've met all my needs. There's never been anyone else; this... just happened." Derek tried to reassure her, but she wasn't buying.

"I'm going to spend the night at my parents," she declared as she began to pack a suitcase. "And I don't know when I'm coming back!"

After Theresa was gone, Derek called Brian.

"Hey, Derek, how are you?" He sounded genuinely glad to get this late night call.

"I'm horrible. I hate to ask this of you, but is there anyway I could see you tomorrow in person? I'll go anywhere you need me to, but I'm desperate."

"No problem, I'm free right after lunch for a couple of

hours. How about the Starbucks on Waters St. in downtown Milwaukee at 1:30?"

"Thank you," Derek was relieved. He felt like Brian would know what to do. He's the one who knew about the crisis before it started.

CHAPTER 15

After a night of tossing and turning, Derek arrived at work a little later than usual. There was a USA Today on his desk with a note from Marie stuck to the paper. The article on the bottom of the front page was headlined: "Micropteryx Finder a Fraud?"

The note from Marie read: "We are all disappointed in you. Harvard is giving me my job back after the funeral. Thanks for nothing."

How had he so misjudged Marie, or was this just what women were like when they were rejected romantically? Derek felt bad for her, but in a way, getting her old job back solved a problem. He wouldn't have to see her, and she wouldn't have to see him every day at work. He didn't even want to read the story about him but felt like the rest of the world would, so he'd better know what it said.

"The incredible find of micropteryx five years ago in Comoros, East Africa, may have been discovered by fraudulent means. World renowned paleontologist, Derek Barnhouse, did not find micropteryx at his own site but at a nearby dig led by Dr. Butch Radcliffe, sources close to both men have revealed. Radcliffe could not be reached for comment, and Barnhouse did not return calls.

The source, who chose to remain anonymous, said that Dr. Barnhouse recently struck a deal with Dr. Radcliffe who recently found out about the foul play. The deal included an undisclosed up front payment as well as all future royalties from Barnhouse's best selling book, The Ascent of Man. It was verified by the publishing company that the royalties are being sent to a new account as of last Friday."

The story was continued on page 5A, but Derek had already seen enough. The whole nation now believed he was a fraud. What would his own children think of him? There was a knock at the door.

"Come in."

David Jackson walked in with a copy of the paper in one hand, and a cup of cappucino in the other.

"I brought this for you," he smiled as he handed him the deluxe mocha. "I thought you might want someone to talk to," he said as he took a seat. "This is horrible," he said holding up the paper. "Do you have any idea who leaked?"

"Yeah, it was Marilyn."

"Marilyn? I'd think she'd be the last person who would want something like this to get out." David seemed astonished at the revelation.

"She's apparently more concerned about what I'm teaching in the classroom than about my reputation. This is her way to keep me in line," Derek explained.

"Is that what the department faculty meeting tomorrow is all about?" David asked.

"Precisely. She wants me to renounce all doubts about macroevolution before the staff to squelch all rumors of me being a heretic."

"What doubts?"

"David, as a geologist, you know all about the uniformitarian view of geology that has been pushed ever since Darwin. And how geologists today, including yourself, are leaning back towards catastrophism because of the facts."

"Yes, I know," Jackson chuckled. "Stone and Becker have been upset because they feel it's opening the door for religious fundamentalism. But we're trying to interpret what is, not what they'd like it to be. Stephen Jay Gould himself said that the infamous Charles Lyell "imposed his imagination upon the evidence" when he wrote the book that helped inspire Darwin. (14) But what's that got to do with macroevolution? I thought that's why you taught Punctuated Equilibrium?"

"It is," Derek answered with hesitancy. "But, is there another possibility? David, have you ever seriously considered special creation? Stone has said all along that punctuated jumps in evolution would be the same biologically as miracles. What if all of the different species are miracles produced by a Creator? What if the reason we can't find any transitory fossils is that there aren't any to find?"

"Now I see why Becker's so uptight," David said with a smile. "Couldn't you just give her the answers she wants to hear and keep your job until the micropteryx thing blows over?"

"I'm seriously considering that," Derek answered. "It's hard for me to tell if I'm really standing on principle or just too proud to give a little."

They sat in silence for a while until David started laughing. "I can't get over the fact that you stole micropteryx right out from under Radcliffe's nose. It's amazing that you pulled it off!"

"Almost pulled it off," Derek corrected. "I already had to pay him a quarter million in cash, as well as signing off on the royalties. Now it looks like I paid him for nothing."

Derek was struggling with despair. "I've got a research assistant doing my afternoon lecture for me, so I can meet with a guy in Milwaukee."

"A lawyer?" David asked.

"No, a philosophy professor who has a lot of insight into people."

CHAPTER 16

Derek was already seated at the Starbucks in downtown Milwaukee when Brian came through the door. After they greeted each other and ordered, Derek poured out all that had happened in the last week.

"So, what are you planning to do at the meeting tomorrow, tell the truth or keep your job?"

"You don't leave much gray area, do you?"

"It seems pretty black and white unless there's something you're not telling me,' Brian questioned with his eyes.

"Hey, I've told you everything. You're the one who's holding back," Derek accused.

"How am I holding back?" asked Brian with sincerity.

"You know more than you're saying. I want to hear everything you know about the dreams and their meaning," Derek insisted.

"Everything?"

"Everything. I've got to know what it all means to face tomorrow."

Brian opened a Bible he pulled out of his backpack and read the passage from Revelation about Jesus again. The image of the glowing silk robe, the gold sash, and the eyes of fire was fresh in Derek's mind as Brian began to comment on it.

"This is a description of the resurrected Christ wearing the robe of a high priest. In the Old Testament the high priest was the one who would enter the Holy of Holies in the temple once a year to offer an atonement, the blood of an innocent animal, for the sins of the people. He entered on behalf of all the people, and as a fellow human being, he could identify with their sin. But he couldn't serve as a permanent mediator because, as a sinful man, he wasn't able to fully identify with the holiness of God.

"Jesus was born on this earth during the Roman empire, but His beginning was from eternity in heaven. He is the second person of the Triune God, the only Son of the Father, who was born on earth so that He could also become a son of man. He is now the only one qualified to be the mediator between heaven and earth because He is fully God and fully man. As our high priest He offered Himself as the sacrifice for our sins, once for all, and is now alive forever to see that His purpose for mankind is realized."

"What purpose? Is that why He's appearing to me in dreams?"

"It's like this, Derek. You've spent your whole life searching for buried treasures, well, now God is seeking after you."

"Why is God so interested in me?" Derek asked. "I don't even go to church."

"The Bible says that God is like a shepherd who leaves ninety-nine sheep in the open pasture to go after the one which is lost, "until he finds it." (Luke 15:4) Simply put, God loves you and wants you to become His child. He's looking for you and I don't think He's going to stop until He finds you."

Derek really did feel like God might be after him. *What a mystery.*

He had one other question that he thought he might as well get out of the way: "Why do you think there was there a gargoyle, or whatever it was right behind me?"

"The first words Satan spoke to the human race were: 'Has God indeed said,'" Brian answered. "He has been casting doubt on God's promises, purposes, and commands ever since. One of his present lies is macroevolution that says that everything is random, and that there is no God lovingly watching over human beings. This world view is contradictory to what the Bible says, and many seem to be on a mission to make people choose between faith and science."

"I've certainly been one of those people. How many young people have been influenced by my lectures and book? If everything you're saying is true, it's frightening how I have been used to mislead people."

"Your life isn't over, Derek," Brian replied. "God wants to redeem you and your life's message, if you'll let Him."

This was all of a sudden too much for Derek. He looked at his watch.

"Thank you, Brian. I really appreciate all the time you've taken with me today," he said as he finished his coffee and started to rise.

Brian took the hint and rose as well. "It was my privilege. Please know that I will be praying for you tonight and tomorrow morning."

"Thank you," Derek replied as he shook hands, said goodbye, and quickly left for Madison.

Derek found a note from Theresa on the dining room table when he returned home.

Derek,

I saw the paper and didn't want the kids to have to deal with it, yet. Dad offered to take us to the Brewers game tonight, and it will go late. We're coming back to their house for a sleep over, so don't look for us.

Theresa

Not "love, Theresa," just, "Theresa." It was the time of his life when he needed her most, and she wasn't here for him. Why were so many bad things happening to him? What had he done wrong to deserve any of this?

As he considered this, a flood of thoughts began to come to him. He had cheated Radcliffe out of micropteryx and justified his behavior. He had flirted with a young, beautiful employee and given in to his passion. He had lived his life to this point without God and without seeking Him in any way. He had promoted an agenda that was contrary to all that God stood for, influencing young, impressionable minds all over the world. Derek decided he wasn't a victim; he was the criminal in God's court.

At this point he began to break. The tears started slowly, and then turned to loud sobs as he got down on his knees, put his face on the floor, and began to pray.

"Dear God, if You're there, please forgive me of my sins and wash away my guilt. Make me whatever you want. I admit that I am lost, please find me."

When the tears finished he felt better, lighter. He went outside and everything seemed brighter and more alive than he remembered. He felt strangely free from his life and his problems in the beauty of all God had made.

He spent the night reading the Bible and enjoying being alone. He wrote Radcliffe, Marie, and Theresa letters of apology. He didn't know if he would send them, but it felt good just to write them. He couldn't remember a night in his life with more peace. For the first time since he was a child, Derek prayed before he went to sleep.

CHAPTER 17

"Thank you for meeting with me so late, David. I didn't know who else to call and I really need to talk." Theresa sat across from David Jackson at the Denny's just off the beltline.

Jackson took a sip of his coffee. "No problem, Theresa. I hadn't turned in yet, and I've been worried about Derek myself. What specifically is bothering you?"

"Do you know about Marie?"

"What about her?" David asked.

Theresa hated to air dirty laundry to one of Derek's friends, but David was her friend as well, and she valued his insight as a man.

"Derek kissed Marie in a hotel room during their trip to Chicago on Monday."

"Really?" Jackson looked shocked. "That doesn't sound like the Derek I know. Who told you about this?"

"He did."

"That's a pretty reliable source," David admitted.

"He told me he stopped after the kiss because he realized how wrong it was, but I still don't know if I can trust him again. Every time I think about it I get angry all over. What if that was the real Derek, and this isn't the first time he's been unfaithful?"

"Hold on, Theresa. Don't you think he would keep it a secret if this was a behavioral pattern? And don't forget that he stopped. Alone with a beautiful young lady, he stopped, and didn't let it progress beyond a kiss."

"Yeah, that's what he says. But I still feel violated."

"Of course you do," David said with genuine compassion in his eyes. "But I think you need to give him another chance. He's been under an enormous amount of stress lately and right now he needs you."

"I know, David. But what do I do with my anger? It feels wrong to pretend it never happened."

"Forgiveness is a gift, but trust is earned," was David's reply.

"What's that supposed to mean?"

"Derek did something that broke your trust in him," David began, "and now he needs the gift of your forgiveness. We all need that gift from time to time."

"Agreed." Theresa grudgingly admitted thinking about her own faults, especially her temper.

"But forgiveness doesn't mean trust," Jackson continued. "It simply provides a new beginning where trust can be earned again."

"So, I can let go of my anger without having to completely drop my guard?" Theresa asked.

"Something like that." David took another drink of his coffee, and Theresa could tell he wanted to say something else.

"What is it, David?"

"I didn't want to share this, but maybe it will help. I was on the verge of an affair early in our marriage," David began. "Claire happened to come to the restaurant where I was having drinks with an adoring grad student. She hit the ceiling."

"But, you two are so in love," Theresa responded with amazement. "I think of your marriage as the goal for ours. What happened?"

"She decided to forgive me, and after enough time I regained her full trust." David now smiled. "We may be even stronger now for having gone through that time."

Theresa was deeply moved. She sat speechless, nursing her decaf, waiting for David to go on.

"You and Derek are a great couple, Theresa. I know you're going to make it." He looked her squarely in the eyes: "Derek needs you now, I think he needs the whole family."

"What do you suggest we do?" she asked with all traces of anger gone from her voice.

"I think you should let me pick you all up tomorrow morning and bring you to the faculty meeting."

"Will they let us in?" Theresa questioned.

"No, but if you stand outside the door you'll hear every word that is spoken, and Derek will know you are there."

Theresa's eyes were now watering as she took David's hand. "We'll do it. Thank you so much, David. You're the best."

CHAPTER 18

*H*e *was looking at the hideous, gargoyle like creature when it turned to him and spoke:*
"You are mine, and so are they."
Derek couldn't speak, and his whole body was now trembling with fear. Shame, despair, and hopelessness filled his mind as the demonic presence breathed its essence all over him.
In desperation, Derek turned, and saw the glowing man across the auditorium. He knew now; it was the Lord. A glimmer of hope began to rise. With anger in His eyes Jesus spoke to the demon: "Let him go!" The words actually formed a sword that went flying through the air in a flash of fire. Derek turned, and the demon was gone.

When Derek woke up he felt a presence of peace all around him. The dream was only a confirmation of what he knew to be true. He was free of the demonic presence that had oppressed him, and was now at the beginning of a new relationship with God. He was a combination of thankful, excited, and afraid. The fear had mainly to do with Theresa, and how she might respond.

When he arrived at the office, it occurred to him how much he loved his job. For ten years he had studied, taught, submitted articles, led digs, and met individually with students. He knew that everything was at risk if he gave the wrong answers in the upcoming meeting.

At ten o'clock the lecture hall they decided to hold the meeting in was packed. Everyone must have delegated their lectures to assistants, because there was not a senior professor from the department absent, except for David Jackson, his one ally. There were many professors from other departments there as well, and to top it off, Chancellor Stoltenmeyer was sitting between Stone and Becker. This was not a good sign. *Where is David?*

"Thank you for taking time out of your busy schedules to be here this morning," Becker began. "I am anticipating a brief meeting. Chancellor Stoltenmeyer, we are honored to have you with us. We appreciate your support and concern for these issues that are vital to all of us. As most of you know there have been some rumors going around about Dr. Barnhouse's beliefs. We all know how things we say can be twisted, so I wanted you to hear from his own lips where he stands. Our faculty is a team and we have to be able to trust each other as well as defend each other when the going gets rough. It has already been a difficult week because of the micropteryx issue, so I'm hoping today's meeting will put everyone's mind at ease. Dr. Barnhouse, please come up front now and take a seat, while I ask you a few questions."

As Derek rose to take his seat and face his peers, he heard the door open in back. It was David, with Theresa, Rachel, and Jared behind him, waving from the hallway as he entered. Derek felt a boost in confidence.

"Dr. Barnhouse, do you believe in an old earth?" Becker started with the anticipated questions.

"I do," was all Derek answered.

"And do you renounce religious dogmatism that puts belief before facts?"

"I do," was, again, all he said.

"And finally, do you hold to macroevolution as the only explanation for everything that exists on our planet?" Derek could see the hope in Becker's eyes as she asked this final question.

It would be so easy to just say "yes." The meeting would be over, he would keep his job, and life would go on. He thought of Theresa and knew that she would be behind him, however he answered. Then he thought about Rachel and Jared. They believed in their Dad, he knew, and were confident that he would tell the truth instead of playing politics. He then allowed himself to think of all the young people around the nation and world who looked to science for the truth. He needed to take a stand no matter what it cost him.

"Dr. Barnhouse?" Becker was now prodding him. "You must answer. Do you still believe in macroevolution?"

"No, I don't," Derek said with a calm that surprised him. "I believe that only microevolution is scientifically proven. I am now convinced macroevolution is about faith."

The gallery was stunned. Quiet at first, and then rising to a low murmur until Becker stood up.

"Silence," she almost yelled with her hand in the air. The room became quiet before she went on. "Thank you for coming today, you are now all dismissed."

"Could we ask professor Barnhouse questions?" Dr. Joe Collins from the philosophy department asked.

Becker was about to shut him down when Chancellor Stoltenmeyer put a hand on her arm and whispered just loud enough so Derek could overhear, "give him his hour. It's the professional thing to do."

"Go ahead," Becker said begrudgingly.

"What about the DNA evidence that links all things together at a molecular level?" Collins asked sincerely.

Derek was surprised that he was given a chance to respond.

"The first question everyone of us needs to ask about DNA is where did it come from? DNA is coded information that is so complex that the amount of information stored within a single nucleus is equal to a library of 1000 encyclopedias, each with 1000 pages. (15) There is no scientific process that can produce information. What if DNA is simply the Divine template of how God made all things? Would intelligent design be proven if every life form had a different molecular system? Or, would that randomness actually be a greater proof for evolution? If there is a Creator, is there a way He could have created that would make you believe in Him?"

Collins was now silent, but another hand went up. Derek nodded at professor Sandra Tompkins.

"Derek, what about all the fossil evidence? You yourself discovered micropteryx, isn't it one of the missing links?"

"The thing about micropteryx," Derek began, "as well as the earlier find of archeopteryx, Sandra, is that it's a fully formed species. Its wings are perfectly suited for flight; its tail is fully formed; and its claws are developed instead of being sharp little stubs. It certainly is a unique being with traits of two different animal classes, much like the duck-billed platypus of today, but it isn't a transitional fossil as much as it is an interesting species. The British Museum of Natural History alone contains some 60 million fossil specimens, yet not one is a transitional form showing one species evolving into another." (16)

Now a third hand went up and began speaking without a prompt. "What about the well documented lineage of mankind? Isn't that proof enough of macroevolution?"

"Let's talk about some of the fossils in that chart," Derek offered with no pride in his voice. "Nebraska Man, the one used to help in the Scopes trial, was revealed in 1927 to be the tooth from an extinct pig.

"Piltdown man was in the chart for forty one years before we realized that the teeth had been filed to fit, and the bones had been stained to make them appear old. Java man is now considered to be a large gibbon and not a human being at all. Peking man was lost during World War II and all we have left is two teeth. And Neanderthal man? He is now thought to be a human who was deformed by age and rickets.(17)

"My friends, after 140 years of looking for missing links, and rewarding only the paleontologists who find them, we have almost nothing that would lead any scientist to think that macroevolution is fact. I am sorry that we have not made our failure to find fossils better known. I think all of us wanted science to have an explanation for everything, but it simply doesn't."

"That's enough!" Becker was on her feet, clearly upset that this discussion was allowed to happen. "You are all dismissed, and expected to keep everything that was talked about here completely confidential."

As professors began to leave she turned to Derek. "Dr. Barnhouse, you will meet with Chancellor Stoltenmeyer and me immediately in your office.

Derek had always been a favorite of Franklin Stoltenmeyer. Kind of like a star quarterback is to a coach, or a high powered salesman is to his boss. On the walk over to Becker's office Derek laughed to himself thinking about a joke he himself had told:

"The coach of a championship team turned to the college president at the awards banquet and asked him a question: 'Would you like me as much if we didn't win all the time?'

"The president thought about it before he answered: 'Of course I would, but we'd sure miss you being around here.'"

This wasn't personal. Franklin was trying to run a university and to do that you needed to maintain your reputation. He was competing for prestige and dollars and no longer had the time or desire to ask hard questions. He knew that Stoltenmeyer had no choice except to fire him.

"Derek, this is very difficult," the chancellor began, "but we can't allow the unethical behavior that you engaged in while on a university sponsored dig in Africa. I'm asking you to pack your stuff up today and not return to this campus."

Becker was nodding. She didn't have a personal agenda against Derek either. If he had answered "yes" to her third question, he had no doubt that she would have made the fraud accusations go away. She was caught in a trap that didn't allow her to rethink what she believed, and the truth was, he felt sorry for her.

"Thanks for all you've done to help me be a success," Derek replied as he shook both of their hands. "I'm sorry it had to end this way. I've enjoyed working here."

The chancellor looked surprised and as if he still wanted to make things right. But there was no way, each of them knew, unless Derek changed his position. They walked out and left him to himself. Once they were gone his family came through the door.

Theresa was still a bit distant, but gave his arm a squeeze. "We are proud of what you did today, Derek."

"You are? Did you know that I'm now unemployed?"

"It doesn't matter, only being together does," she said with tears in her eyes.

Jared gave him a hug. "You were the man in there, Dad."

Then Rachel approached him, glowing with love and with a tear on her cheek. "You are a Braveheart," she said as she gave him a hug and whispered, "I love you, Daddy."

EPILOGUE

"So what are we going to do now?" Jared asked his dad as the family sat by the pool the evening after the faculty meeting.

"I don't know, Jared."

"Where are we going to live?" Jared looked bewildered.

"I don't know that either," Derek answered. "The Century 21 agent said he would be out today to put the 'For Sale' sign up on the house. Hopefully, we'll have some answers by the time this place sells."

"I guess it's called a life of faith for a reason," offered Rachel with a half smile.

Theresa looked contemplative. "What time do the Patricks arrive?"

"I told them the steaks would be on the grill by 5:30," Derek replied as he looked at his watch. "I've actually never met the rest of Brian's family. His wife's name is Leslea, and I guess they have four kids, from college to toddler. They'll be here in force."

"Well, I've got some questions for Brian," Theresa stated. "If we're going to do this 'by faith' thing, I want to talk to someone who's been on the journey for more than two weeks."

Derek chuckled. "It seems crazy doesn't it. I've spent my

whole life observing and explaining things we can see, and now we're dedicating our future to the leadership of Someone we can't see."

"How can you be so sure God is leading us, Dad?" Jared asked. "What if God doesn't care that you lost your job or about where we're going to live?"

"It's hard to explain," Derek began. "And I don't think I can give you a good logical reason, but I just know He cares. It's like this, Jared: Once I find a fossil that I have searched for with painstaking effort, I make sure that it is protected and cared for. God has surprisingly gone out of His way to find me, so why would He abandon us now?"

Derek's cell phone rang. He didn't recognize the number.

"Hello, this is Derek Barnhouse."

"Doctor Barnhouse, this is Elaine Blake from UCLA."

"President Blake, how can I help you?"

"I just got off the phone with Franklin Stoltenmeyer," she began.

"Really?" was all Derek could manage back.

"He spoke very highly of you in spite of the fraud accusations, and your doubts about macroevolution. I'm calling today, Derek, to ask you a question that might change the rest of your life."

Derek couldn't help laughing at her reference to his lecture. "And what would that question be?" he finally replied.

"How would you like to interview at UCLA?"

AUTHOR'S NOTE

Many years ago I read a book by Phillip E. Johnson called "Darwin on Trial," that exposes the lack of proof for macroevolution. I've encouraged people to read it, usually by mailing them a copy, but only the most passionate about science ever do.

Recently our church board gave me a study leave to prepare for a series of lectures I did in our community called, "Evolution, Science, and the Bible." It was fulfilling to do the study and share it with the eighty to a hundred people that came, but I realized that the people who needed this material the most, would be the least likely to read the manual I put together, or listen to the CDs we recorded.

Then I read Proverbs 15:2 out of the New Living Translation: "The wise person makes learning a joy." Why not take the material and put it into a story that young people would enjoy? All of the quotes and facts in this book were from the lectures. If you want to order the CDs, e-mail: office@ montecbc.com and we'd be happy to mail them to you.

I am grateful to Dwight Clough, Brian White, and my daughter Annie who all helped edit, and to my other children for their willingness to hear the story chapter by chapter and tell me forthright what wouldn't work. A special thanks to my Mom, who helped finance the project, and to my wife, Alice, for encouraging me even though it meant time away from her.

God bless you,
Tom Flaherty

APPENDIX

There are two Hebrew words used in Genesis chapter one that are important to understand if we're going to interpret Exodus 20:11; 'bara' and 'asah.' 'Bara' means to create from nothing and is used for only three things in Genesis one; once in relation to the heavens and the earth in verse one, then in relation to the animals in verse 21, and finally for mankind in verse 27.

The other word, 'asah', means 'to do,' or 'to make from preexisting materials.' Bara is translated 'created' while asah is translated 'made.' Notice that it is before the seven days that God created the heavens and the earth. When God 'made' the expanse on day two He didn't create anything, He just reorganized what was already there. He separated the water below from the water above, and called the air inbetween, 'heaven.'

When He 'made' the earth in verse three He didn't create anything either. He gathered the waters together and called them 'seas,' and the dry land that appeared He called 'earth.' It was the same way when He 'made' the sun, moon, and the stars in verse 16. He didn't create anything new, He just pulled back the cloud cover and brought the heavenly bodies forth, so they could be viewed on earth.

Job 38:4-8 tells us that after creating the earth God made

a 'cloud its garment, and thick darkness its swaddling band.' Notice in Genesis 1:2 it says that darkness was on the face of the deep. Darkness covered only the face of the earth; the rest of the universe was shining brightly since the stars were already created in verse one. The thick clouds that caused this darkness dispersed enough on day one to produce the first solar day on earth, 'evening and morning.' But it is not until day four that the cloud cover is completely removed so that the stars could be viewed from this earth. It takes millions of years for many stars' light to even reach the earth. If they had been created on day four of the present creation, we still wouldn't see them.

When Exodus 20:11 says that God 'made' the heavens and the earth and the sea, it uses the word 'asah' referring to the work God did during the six days when God made the expanse and called it 'heaven;' made dry land appear and called it 'earth;' and gathered the waters calling them 'seas.'" God created the heavens and the earth sometime in the distant past; He later judged Satan's rebellion; and then He worked for six days on the earth to prepare it for a new creation, mankind. And then He rested from all His work.

END NOTES

Chapter 3

1 James Perloff, "Time Magazine's New Age-Man," Creation Matters, Vol. 6, No. 4, July/August 2001, 2.

Chapter 5

2 Origin of the Species (Penguin Library Edition, 1982) as quoted in Darwin on Trial, Phillip Johnson (Intervarsity Press: Downers Grove, Illinois, 1993), 47.
3 Ibid, 46
4 Ibid, 50
5 Ibid, 59
6 Ibid, 59

Chapter 6

7 Ron Carlson, Christian Ministries International, tape 2 "Fossils, Dinosaurs, and Geology," 2001.
8 World Magazine, Asheville, North Carolina, February 7, 2004, 15.
9 Florence Raulin-Cerceau, "From Panspermia to bioastronomy: The Evolution of the Hypothesis of Universal

Life," Origins of Life and Evolution of the Biosphere, 1998, 597.

10 The Autobiography of Charles Darwin (New York: Harcourt, Brace and Company, 1958), 85.

11 Darwin on Trial, 33.

Chapter 11

12 New International Version, 1973, 1.

13 Darwin on Trial, 57.

Chapter 15

14 Stephen Jay Gould, Ever Since Darwin, 150. Quoted from Darwin on Trial.

Chapter 16

15 Richard Simmons, "What Darwin Didn't Know, Harvest House, Eugene, Oregon, 2004, 30.

16 Hank Hanegraff, "Face the facts about evolution," statement DF803, Christian Research Institute.

17 Grant Jeffrey, "Creation," Frontier Research Publications, Inc, 2003, 210.

Printed in the United States
112493LV00002B/105/A